RAGS TO WITCHES

SOUTHERN RELICS COZY MYSTERIES

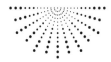

BELLA FALLS

EVERMORE PRESS

CONTENTS

Southern Relics Cozy Mysteries

Flea Market Magic: Book 1

Rags To Witches: Book 2

Pickup and Pirates

A Southern Charms Cozy Mystery Series

Moonshine & Magic: Book 1

Lemonade & Love Potions (Southern Charms Cozy Short)

Fried Chicken & Fangs: Book 2

Sweet Tea & Spells: Book 3

Barbecue & Brooms: Book 4

Collards & Cauldrons: Book 5

Cornbread & Crossroads: Book 6 (Coming Soon)

*All audiobooks available are narrated by the wonderful and talented Johanna Parker

For a FREE exclusive copy of the prequel to the Southern Charms series, Chess Pie & Choices, sign up for my newsletter - https://dl.bookfunnel.com/opbg5ghpyb

Share recipes, talk about Southern Charms and all things cozy mysteries, and connect with me by joining my reader group Southern Charms Cozy Companions - https://www.facebook.com/groups/southerncharmscozycompanions/

CHAPTER ONE

G iggles gurgled up from my insides like the bubbles in my second glass of champagne. Cate and my cousin Dani joined me, cackling at Crystal trying on some paisley monstrosity from another decade.

"Ms. Robin, I just can't believe you made this." The bell sleeves of the blouse fluttered in the air like wings sprouting out of Crystal's sides. "Or that anyone actually used to wear anything like it."

"Hey, Robin Westwood Designs were worn by some of the biggest names at the time," Cate defended. "We're so lucky to have someone with her incredible talent anywhere close to us. I don't think we could have afforded a big bridal trip to NYC."

"Yeah, well, thank goodness she keeps up with

the changes in style over time. Because this is just way too groovy for me." Crystal busted out her best disco moves.

Watching her attempts at dancing cracked me up. My laugh mixed with a sneeze that rocked my entire body, and I fell off the couch, spilling the drink all over my sundress.

Tara, the wedding shop's assistant and a new coven friend, dashed out of the dressing area at the sound of the commotion. "Oh my stars, are you okay?" When she noticed my wet front, she hurried off to find a towel for me.

The curtain pulled back from the smaller dressing room, and all three of my friends joined me in oohing over our friend Gloria stepping into view with the most gorgeous dress hugging her body. The violet hues of the delicate fabric accented her every move.

Crystal wolf whistled at our friend. "Girl, I don't think I've ever seen you look better."

Dani nodded in agreement. "You're definitely going to have a real shot at bagging one of the groomsmen that's *not* your brother."

"You think?" Gloria turned left and right, regarding her reflection. "The only time I can remember looking better was the night I finally caught Harrison's attention. Remember that, Rue?"

Even with my head a little fuzzy, I would never forget my friend and former co-worker's efforts to get our fellow bartender to stop seeing her as his best friend's little sister and to drool over the hot woman she'd turned into.

"Ironically, that required you to have a whole lot less clothing on, whereas I think you look even hotter all dolled up." I burped and giggled some more. Cupping my hands to my mouth, I lowered my voice, "If I didn't know better, I'd swear Ms. Robin was a witch. She has to use magic when she sews."

Crystal snatched the almost empty flute out of my grasp. "Why don't you say it a little louder in a shop run by a mortal." Offering me her hand, she helped me to my feet before smacking me upside the head.

"Huh. I thought I was whispering." I blinked and asked the rest of our party, "Wasn't I whispering?"

Tara returned with a towel for me to wipe off my dress and one to clean up the mess I'd created. Feeling a little guilty, I offered to wipe it up myself, but she waved me off. "I've got it." She checked to see who was around and lowered her voice, "And you're not the only one who thinks Ms. Robin has a special touch with her sewing. Even I spent my first month on the job trying to test her to see if she had any actual hidden powers. It's ironic that today, she's the only one in the place without any."

Gloria, still busy gawking at her reflection in the mirror while listening to our conversation, ran her hands over her bridesmaid's dress. "She definitely has a special talent with fabric though, turning it from strips of woven threads into beautiful creations. I think that's its own magic."

"Why, thank you, darling." Ms. Robin stepped out of the bigger dressing room. Unlike her amazing creations surrounding us, the older lady wore her gray hair in a tight bun with escaped tendrils framing her face and a simple neutral-colored outfit made for comfort rather than fashion. "What a sweet compliment, although you have to give credit where it's due. Gloria's finishes on your dress are exceptional."

Our fellow coven member and shop assistant blushed. "Thanks, Ms. Robin."

"No, dear, thank you. With wedding season bearing down on us, I don't know what I'd do without you." The talented seamstress and designer turned to face the rest of us. "Now, who's ready to see the bride?"

Forcing Cate and Dani to scooch over, I plopped down next to my friends on the couch and leaned forward in anticipation. Moving with care in her dress, Gloria perched on the arm of the couch to give her best friend the floor. We all clapped in anticipation and waited for the big reveal. Tara and Ms. Robin pulled back the velvet curtains and watched us for our reaction.

"Oh, Azalea. You look absolutely stunning," Gloria gushed, sniffing to hold back tears.

The rest of us stared at the bride-to-be in silent appreciation. She approached us, holding a bouquet of fake flowers and wearing a delicate tiara with a gauzy veil attached to it.

Dani and I hummed the bridal march, and a beaming smile spread across Azalea's face. "Do y'all really like it? I had to fight to get what I really wanted. If my mother had her way, I'd be in something as white as a snowy egret with poufy sleeves and a ridiculously big skirt. Thank goodness Ms. Robin here helped me wrangle her so I could have this dress."

"What did you do?" I queried.

The store owner shrugged. "What was absolutely

needed. I reminded her mother that it was Azalea's big day and not hers. That fashions have changed over time." She raised a critical eyebrow at Crystal, still wearing the 70's top. "And that if she wasn't willing to get onboard, she could leave."

Her statement caused our mouths to drop. "You kicked out the mother of the bride?" asked Dani, her eyes widened in awe.

"No, not really," countered Azalea. "She's aware of the design we came up with, but I wanted her to be surprised with everyone else on the actual day with everything finished. The only thing that might make them a little upset is the color." Her eyes flashed to Ms. Robin's. "Do you think the slight pink of the dress will upset them?"

Gloria approached her friend, took the fake bouquet away from her to hand off to Tara, and held her hands. "Anyone who knows you knows what your favorite color has always been. Heck, if you'd given into your mom and had a white dress made, I would have been right there with you to dye it pink myself."

Azalea sighed, and her shoulders relaxed a little. "I knew you were my best friend for a reason. For your support and for setting me up with one of your exes."

Gloria blew out a breath in dismissal. "Harrison was barely an ex. We had three dates and one kiss and knew immediately we had no real chemistry. But I knew he could show a girl a good time, which is why I encouraged you to go out with him. You know, to dust off the cobwebs from your dating life. It never occurred to me that you'd be the one to tame the tomcat right out of him. And look at you now." She spread her friend's arms wide. "The most beautiful bride in the world."

"Give us a good runway walk," I called out.

Azalea chuckled and slouched in a dramatic fashion, pouting in her best imitation of a model. She strutted back and forth in front of us.

Ms. Robin played along with pleasure. "Here we see our bride in a V-neck trumpet tulle wedding gown with cap sleeves. The blush hue compliments her skin tone and reminds us of her flowery personality while the fabric flows down her body like a lazy river, moving with fluidity every step she takes. The lace flowers of the structured bodice continue down the tulle skirt in cascades, accentuating the botanical theme of the entire wedding."

Dani sighed with a goofy grin. "You look like a fairy princess."

I gave the bride two thumbs up and a hiccup.

"Harrison is going to lose it when he sees you walking down the aisle at your venue. The Wallace House will be the perfect place."

To none of our surprise, Azalea had managed to pull off booking the best place in the whole area. She would get married in the gardens under a flower-covered trellis and then hold an amazing reception afterwards at tables that lined the backyard while the sun set over the Bogue Sound. As long as the weather stayed nice, it would be an amazing night for everyone there.

Tara cleared her throat, interrupting our gushes of admiration. "Excuse me, Ms. Robin, but I think maybe we should help these two ladies out of their dresses before anything happens to them."

The older fashion designer dismissed her with a wave of her hand. "I suppose you're right. Sometimes it's nice to stop and admire one's work when it turns out so well. This dress will go down as one of my greatest masterpieces."

"You mean I'm not wearing one myself?" Crystal held up her arm to flutter the sleeves of the paisley top.

The seamstress scowled for a half-second before letting my friend off with a wink. "I'll have you know that fashions go in and out of style all the time. Just you wait, that top will be a desired item again someday. In the meantime, be careful when you take it off," she chided, pointing at the half-naked mannequin.

With care, Crystal peeled off the flowing fabric. "Come on, Ms. Robin. We've heard a few stories about when you were a famous designer all those years in New York before you walked away from it all and moved down here. I can't believe you gave up the life of a rich and famous clothes designer."

The lady clicked her tongue in dismissal. "All the fame and fortune in the world wouldn't give me half of what my Buster did. All I needed was him and my sewing machine to live a happy life." She turned to give her full attention to Azalea, stepping forward and cupping her chin. "Sweet child, the best thing I could wish for you is to be as lucky in love as Buster and I were in all of your future choices. It doesn't take a pretty dress to be successful at that. Although it sure doesn't hurt to start off your journey together looking as beautiful as you do."

Azalea's cheeks blushed to match the color of her dress. "Thanks, Ms. Robin. That's a truly wonderful blessing and compliment."

Multiple sniffs filled the air, and I dashed my knuckle under my eye to catch a stray tear. "If we're this sentimental at a dress fitting, we'd better invest in boxes of tissues for the actual event."

"Do you want me to assist you in getting Miss Azalea out of her dress?" Tara interrupted with a touch of impatience that snapped the rest of us out of our girly wedding haze.

The seamstress ignored her assistant's tone with an easy smile. "Actually, we can do this quicker if a couple of you will help both of us. Then we can get Azalea and Gloria changed so you ladies can get on with the rest of your day."

Positive I'd be all thumbs and rip something in my slightly inebriated state, I stayed out of the dressing area and helped to clean up our bridal group mess. Placing the fluted glasses on a tray, I relied on my old bartender skills to keep them steady as I carried them to the back room where they kept their cakes and other bottles of bubbly for customers tucked away.

After rinsing out the glasses and washing the last of the crumbs off the plates, I wiped my hands off with a nearby towel and went back out onto the showroom. With everyone else still occupied with helping the bride-to-be and her bridesmaid, I took my time walking around the room to admire the stitched handiwork. Tara was right to test Ms. Robin for any sense of her possessing magic. The woman had some serious talent in creating clothes.

A row of mannequins on the far side of the room showed off what must have been old fashion designs from the seamstress's days up North. The ones in the front shop windows displayed gorgeous variations of formal dresses. A certain handsome vampire came to mind while I inspected the rows of hanging wedding dresses. I pictured what I'd look like standing next to Luke under a trellis full of flowers wearing each style. Would he like me in lace? Or maybe beads and sequins? One particular one with feathers adorning the entire skirt of the dress made me chortle, and I dismissed wanting to look like a swan when my day came with a shake of my head.

"By my estimation, you'd want something a little less edgy and more classic," Ms. Robin said, inter-rupting my fantasies. "Has your boyfriend popped the question yet? He certainly spends a lot of money on his vintage cars. Surely he can throw a little at a diamond for you."

If only she knew exactly how much wealth my vampire boyfriend had amassed over his centuries of living. Heck, he could probably buy me a thousand diamonds if he wanted to. Or maybe he owned a few expensive baubles wherever he hid his assets.

Getting a ring wouldn't be a problem. Having him actually *give* me one? Now, that would be my biggest challenge.

Ever since I'd tasted his blood to help defeat whatever evil lived inside the crystal ball I'd found, he'd stopped even teasing me with the possibility of marriage. An unknown chasm had opened between us, and despite my efforts, I hadn't been able to figure out what had happened or how to close the gap that seemed to widen with each day.

My friends gathered around me in time to watch my face fall into a scowl. Dani hugged my shoulders and kissed my forehead. "Best not to ask that question, Ms. Robin. My cousin tends to get a little surly when you do."

I pushed her off of me. "Do not," I grumbled.

The rest of the ladies present laughed at my reaction that proved her point. Heat rose in my cheeks. "No, he hasn't asked me." *Yet*. Forcing myself to recover, I plastered a grin on my face. "But when he does, I'll be sure to come shopping here for my dress."

"Well, you'd better hope he asks you sooner rather than later. I have plans to close the shop at some point in the next year." The older woman straightened a row of hanging dresses, avoiding the collective gasps.

"You didn't tell me that," Tara uttered, her eyes widened as much as my own.

Ms. Robin realized her slip up and glanced back at her assistant with regret. "I know we haven't had that particular talk yet. We'll definitely have more conversations about it, but I think you're talented enough to get out there and start making it on your own. And you know you'll have my recommendation to back you up on your journey."

A cloud passed over Tara's face, but she shook it off and attempted to recover. "Well, at least I've had the opportunity to train under you for the past year."

Gloria stepped forward. "And if you're responsible for my dress, then I have to say you're going to make one heck of a designer on your own."

Our friend's compliment saved the day. "Thank you," Tara murmured, leaving us and disappearing into the back room.

Ms. Robin grimaced. "I stepped my foot in it, but sometimes the mother hen has to kick the baby bird out of the nest, or something like that." She escorted us to the door and patted Azalea's arm. "Tara and I will arrive early to the bridal suite at the Wallace

House to help you get dressed on your day. You've got nothing to worry about."

After we said our goodbyes, we solidified the bachelorette night plans before splitting up. Before getting in my truck, I grabbed Dani and headed back inside, a different kind of plan percolating in my head.

"Oh, sweetie, did you forget something?" Ms. Robin asked.

Breathless, I made my request. "I don't suppose you might have something classic that I could wear to the wedding?" If I could look my absolute best on Azalea's big day, then maybe Luke would take notice. A dress might not fix everything, but maybe I could kindle enough heat to remind him of the good that existed between us.

The seamstress tapped her lip with her finger. "How much is your budget?"

Although I wasn't rich, I did well enough. And what price would I pay to Luke drool? "No limits."

Dani gasped and bumped my hip with hers. "Really? You willing to empty your savings for a dress?"

Her question chilled my enthusiasm. "Well, maybe not more than a few hundred. I can eat stale cornbread in milk or mayo and banana sandwiches for a while if it means I'll knock my boyfriend's socks right off."

Dani rolled her eyes. "You know I'll never let you starve. You can eat anytime you want at the Rise & Shine. I'm not here to rain on your parade. Guess I'm just surprised you would spend so much on something for yourself."

Doubt doused my excitement. "Maybe you're right. How can one dress fix everything?"

Ms. Robin rushed to my side and took me by the crook of my arm. "Do *not* underestimate the magic of a well-fitted dress. Come with me. I know I've got at least a couple here that I think will change your mind."

CHAPTER TWO

I followed the banging of cupboards and clanging of pots into my kitchen and collapsed onto a chair at the small table, praying for death. Dani waved a strip of bacon in front of my nose, and I snatched it out of her hand only to chuck it back at her.

"Hey, it's a Southern sin to waste bacon. It's not my fault you overdid it last night," she chastised, rescuing the crispy slice and munching on it.

I lowered my head onto the cool wood surface and emitted a long, painful moan. The stilted shuffling of feet and two more chairs scraping the floor alerted me to my other friends and their reluctant presence.

"Good mornin', ladies!" my cousin shouted at the

newcomers with way too much glee, setting a plate of ooey gooey cinnamon rolls in the middle of our pathetic group.

Crystal and Cate replied with their own declarations of woe. Out of solidarity, I managed enough energy to lift up my hand to flip Dani the bird.

My cousin popped the back of my head with a spatula. "Y'all are gonna need to eat if you want to start feeling better so we can enjoy the wedding today."

Placing my elbows on the table, I propped my head up with both hands. "There better not be bacon grease in my hair," I warned her and winced at my loud tone.

"Be nice or I won't make you toad-in-a-hole eggs," Dani threatened. "And you girls? What kind can I whip up for you? Over easy? Scrambled?" She pointed the spatula at all of us barely holding it together.

Crystal groaned and tried to run her fingers through the bird's nest of hair on top of her head. "If I had the energy, I would hex your chirpy behind right now." After her fingers got caught in the tangled tresses, she gave up and poured all of us deep cups of coffee. "Thank goodness my husband isn't seeing me like this. I don't think I've been this wasted in a long time."

"Yeah, it should be against the law for anyone to be lookin' like you are right now. I don't think you partied right," accused Cate with a pointed finger, blinking at my cousin with blurry eyes outlined by smudged mascara and eye liner. "Remind me again how we ended up participating in a kind of impromptu second bachelorette party last night?" she asked, reaching for a cinnamon bun off the full plate in the middle of the table and taking a bite.

I tapped the side of my mouth to alert her to the big glob of frosting hanging from her lip. "If you'd overheard what Azalea's parents said to her at her own rehearsal dinner, I think you would have sided with me and Gloria that she needed to blow off some steam."

"Her parents didn't really offer to pay her *not* to marry Harrison, did they?" Dani stopped fussing over the food, her expression full of sympathy and disbelief.

"Heard it myself when I went to go thank Gus, the owner of Spinner's, for putting together such an amazing seafood meal for the families. They'd cornered her on the way to the bathroom." I grimaced at the memory of their hushed tones of judgment and the pounding of my head.

"You should check on Azalea. Or maybe with Gloria. See if everything's okay," my cousin suggested, placing a plate in front of me with two slices of bread with the crusts cut off and eggs perfectly fried up in the middle. The two yellow yolks stared back at me in judgment of my current state.

"We should have cut ourselves off when you did, Dani Jo. I think we might regret not following your fine example last night." With one finger, I typed out a text on my spell phone and waited. I winced at the quiet chime apprising me of the incoming reply. "Gloria says that she and Azalea are at the pre-wedding breakfast with Azalea's mother and the other bridesmaids. No apparent drama in the light of day."

"Wow," Crystal exclaimed. "That's impressive that they're both fine."

I read the next text that pinged. "They're not. Gloria claims Azalea's amazing skills with makeup helps them to look livelier than they are, and that there's not enough magic in the world to kill her hangover headache, even though she swears she made sure they both drank a lot of water and took some medicine before passing out." The phone chimed again. "And a little sneaky hair of the dog in their coffee."

"I just can't believe Azalea's parents. I mean, who tries to bribe the bride not to get married the day before their wedding? That's cold on a whole other level," exclaimed Crystal.

"I asked Gloria for more details when I filled her in somewhere between the drinks at Tortugas and the Tiki. She said that Azalea's been fighting with them on and off since the engagement. They think she could do better than a bartender." Having served as one myself before joining the family business, that sentiment burned my behind.

Crystal scoffed. "He's moved up to manager and has talked about investing in the place or even opening up his own bar on the beach."

Cate snapped her fingers. "Wait, is that why her parents seemed cold and aloof at their binding ceremony with the coven? Because he's not a witch either?"

Based on the expletives that exploded out of Gloria's mouth when she'd confessed all the dirty details of the riff between the bride and her parents, I knew exactly where they stood with their daughter getting hitched to a mortal.

I wiped my hand down my face. "Let's just say I'm amazed at how well Azalea's managed to stay so upbeat this entire time. Gloria's doing her absolute best to get her down the aisle and keep her from going off the rails. Last night was my attempt to achieve the same goal."

"Yeah, but whose idea was it to turn a glass of wine into a full-blown beach bar blowout?" Crystal groaned, rubbing the sides of her temples.

Dani cracked an egg in the skillet. "I thought it was fun revisiting all of the places we used to frequent and recall funny stories. Y'all were the ones who guzzled all that booze." At the mention of drinks, I did a quick mental calculation of how much we'd consumed.

"Why are you turning green in the face?" Cate asked.

I squeezed my eyes shut. "I stupidly tallied up the shots and amount of drinks we must have had last night."

"Stop! No good can come from going down that long, twisted path to destruction," insisted Crystal, holding up her mug of coffee. "Here's hoping today will go off without any problems."

Dani placed a plate of scrambled eggs for sharing in between the two girls. "You better hope she didn't pick up some actual jinx when Harrison saw her last night."

I stopped chewing and tried to clear the fog of drunkenness from my brain. "That's right. He did show up at the Tiki. Said he'd forgotten something there that he needed for the wedding."

"Oh, yeah." Cate giggled, careful not to spill coffee on her. "You two hilariously tried to cover up Azalea with your bodies and ended up knocking her on her behind."

Crystal and I pointed at each other and shouted at the same time, "It was her fault." The entire table of my girlfriends cackled at the recovered recollection.

"And it was after midnight. The groom wasn't supposed to see the bride on the day of the wedding. We were trying to protect her from tempting fate and earning any bad luck," I explained. "If our balance hadn't been shot to heck, we might have been more effective."

Harrison had declared us menaces to society before pushing Crystal and me off of his fiancée and lifting Azalea to her feet. It took the rest of us begging to convince him to leave his soon-to-be-bride with us for her big finale. In the bright light of the morning, I wondered if she wouldn't have been better off letting him take her home after the rehearsal dinner instead of coming out with us.

"I think Azalea may have more to deal with than worrying about bad luck from Harrison seeing her last night," I insisted. After a second, I added, "And if her parents try anything, maybe we can hex their mouths shut."

Dani tossed a piece of egg at me. "Don't even joke about that. If you use magic against a fellow coven member without a formal challenge, they could kick you out."

I shrugged. "It might be worth it when the recipients are acting like they are." Thoughts of what my own family thought of Luke and wondering how they'd treat him if we ever got so far as a wedding distracted me into silence.

We forced ourselves to eat some of my cousin's excellent cooking. Quiet moans of pain turned into grunts of acceptance and even a little pleasure by the time food filled our bellies and chased away our hangovers.

Buoyed by food and conversation, we finished up our breakfast and made plans to meet up to sit together at the wedding later in the afternoon. Dani stayed to help clean my kitchen despite my protests, but her cheerful spirit helped me to deny my instincts to wallow and to pull up my big girl britches to get on with my day.

"How are things with Luke?" she dared to ask, probably guessing where my thoughts had headed with all the wedding talk.

Having confided more to her than anyone else in the family, I relied on her take of the truth to help. "It's not that he isn't a good boyfriend. He is. But there's been this consistent distance between us ever since the effects of me tasting his blood wore off."

Luke hadn't been kidding with his warning that consuming even a drop of his blood to help enhance my own magic would be tough. It had helped me defeat whatever was living in the crystal ball that night, but it had also messed with my general senses. I had no idea how he'd lived for so long when he could hear things amplified in volume or at a distance of hundreds of feet away. Smell my aunt's baking at the cafe that sat at the edge of our property. Pick up on people's emotions before they were even aware of what they felt.

At first, I'd reveled in the extra abilities, feeling a little like a superhero. They definitely came in handy when picking and scrounging for used goods. Uncle Jo and my father had showered compliments on me for my finds and savvy bargain hunting. About two weeks ago, I noticed the effects finally waning when the constant chirping of cicadas in the evening soothed me rather than drove me up the wall with the volume of their rhythmic song.

"If you could see the way he looks at you, you'd know how much he's in love. That man would do anything for you." Dani tossed the damp dishcloth onto the counter and pulled me into a hug.

I rested my head on her shoulder, desperately willing tears not to fall. "I do know that deep down."

It wasn't his love I didn't trust. I couldn't shake the suspicion that he was hiding something from me. Or maybe it was the wall he threw up when I pressed my newfound powers to try and sense more about him. Whatever big secret he kept locked away had caused the kernel of worry to take seed. And when my extra powers faded, his insistence that everything was normal fertilized my doubt.

My cousin rubbed my back. "When he sees you all dolled up in that dress you bought, I'll bet you'll definitely know how he feels about you. There's no way he's going to let anyone else dance with you tonight."

"Best money I've spent in a long time," I admitted, squeezing her one last time and letting her go with a sniff.

"Now, no waterworks except for what's in the sink." Dani splashed me with the dirty dishwater, and I answered her by soaking her T-shirt with wet sloshes of my own.

A knock on the door interrupted our soapy water fight, and I grabbed the damp dish towel and wiped myself off as best I could. Dani answered the door and escorted Ms. Robin into my humble abode.

The talented designer carried a garment bag in her hands. "Good morning, ladies."

"Ms. Robin, I wasn't expecting *you* to drop off my dress. I thought Tara was going to do it," I exclaimed, clearing the way for her to come inside.

The older lady sighed with a smile. "When I talked to her this morning, I surmised she might have had a little *too* much fun with you girls last night. Ah, to be young and foolish." She handed me the bag. "I sent her to the Wallace House to set up the bridal suite with everything we might need to get Azalea and the rest of the bridesmaids ready. I like for everything to run as smoothly as possible and for the bride to want for absolutely nothing on her special day."

Dani hugged me around my waist. "Aww. I can't wait to get married so you can design my dress."

"Well, sweetheart, you better get a move on

quick. I stopped by to talk with your daddy about consigning some of my stuff once I close the shop for good as I was driving back here." She frowned. "Strange thing, though. A big rooster about the size of a small dog interrupted us and chased Jo around the yard."

Dani and I exchanged knowing glances, and I snorted. "Everyone's afraid of Rex the Rooster. He's decided that he not only gets to strut his stuff with our new chickens, it's also his job to guard the barns. He gives our cat Buddy, and anybody else trying to get into them, all kinds of problems," I explained, leaving out the part that Rex only tolerated Deacon, my cousin and Dani's brother, who'd been cursed into giant pig form by a scorned witch he tried dating once.

"Well, one of you girls tell your fathers that I'd like someone from your family to come after hours to the shop and evaluate what I have." A cloud of sadness passed over her face. "It'll be one of the hardest things I'll ever do, letting my old sewing machine go. I used it for some of my very first jobs. Even now, every dress I make has some part of it sewn by her."

Sympathy flooded my heart. "You can always keep the sewing machine with you."

"No, as long as she keeps working, she needs to belong to someone who will use her to make beautiful things for others." Ms. Robin flexed her hands in front of her. "I wish I could do this job for the rest of my life, but…" she trailed off. With a sniff, she shook her head and shifted moods while she took her leave. "Oh well, no point in being so maudlin on a day like today. I think the weather's going to be perfect for tonight's event."

"I hope it is," I added, glancing out the open door at the brightened sky. "But rain or shine, I'm gonna look amazing in your dress."

"It's your dress now, darling, and I hope it brings you much happiness." Ms. Robin waved at Dani and me. "See you two at the reception. I think it's going to be an unforgettable event."

CHAPTER THREE

For the hundredth time during the wedding, I wiped a tear away as Azalea and Harrison walked down the aisle as officially husband and wife. Their joyful faces beamed at everyone when they weren't glancing with absolute delight at each other.

I clutched my hand over my heart. "That was a beautiful ceremony."

Luke leaned against me and whispered in my ear, "It has to be a sin that you look better than the bride." His heated eyes raked over my body with appreciation, and I made a mental note to do something special for Ms. Robin in gratitude for my incredible dress.

"Thank goodness for waterproof mascara." Dani

pulled a tissue out of her clutch purse and dabbed at her eyes.

Crystal sighed. "You'd better give me one of those, too. Sweet tea and spells, I thought I was going to lose it during Harrison's vows." She patted her husband Odie's arm. "Don't worry, honey, your vows were perfectly good enough that I'm still married to you," she teased, quickly kissing his bearded cheek after her joke.

"See, this is why I know they're right for each other," I interjected with a sniff. "Before he met Azalea, there's no way I would believe he could compose anything like that. I kinda feel bad for all the men here tonight."

Luke raised an eyebrow at me. "Why?"

I winked at my girlfriends. "Because y'all will have to raise your games now that Harrison set the bar so high."

We filtered out of our row of seats along with the rest of the guests to allow for the professional photographer to take some pictures with the bridal party. When I paused to watch the group assembling into place, the sour expressions from Azalea's parents caught my attention. Gloria spotted me spying and rolled her eyes behind their heads and shrugged. I waved at her, wishing her supportive luck from afar.

While most of the guests mingled for cocktails in a designated bar area, my girls and I left our men and snuck into the reception area to peek at all of Azalea's hard work and planning put into action. Although her family could afford the very best in wedding preparations, the bride wanted to add her own personal touch and try to do as much as she could on her own to save a little bit of money. Any professional wedding designer would have been awed by the decorations all of us had helped her create over the last few months.

Mason jars with tea light candles glowing inside hung from white lights strung over the guest tables. They matched the ones included in the centerpieces filled with a mix of wildflowers and sprigs of gorgeous bouquets of pink and lavender from a local florist. A magnolia flower and leaf in front of every plate cradled individual place cards with the guest names scrawled in impeccable calligraphy.

"Wow, when Azalea said she wanted Southern chic, I never had this in mind." Cate examined one of the flowers of a nearby table centerpieces. With a slight smile, she cradled a flower nestled between sweet honeysuckle vines, leaned in, and whispered to the pink blossom. It brightened and bloomed a little more, settling into the floral design as its beautiful star.

"I just love your touch with nature." I hugged her shoulders. "Had I tried something like that, it probably would have shriveled up and died."

"Your fire magic doesn't exactly blend well with my earth talents. No sense in setting the flowers ablaze. But you could help out with the candles." She pointed me in the direction of a few darkened jars.

"I'm on it." Happy to be able to help with something, I cast a few small spells to make sure all of the candles would burn brightly until the celebration ended.

As I finished casting a lasting flame at another mason jar, I flinched at the sound of someone clearing their throat. "I would appreciate it if you wouldn't flaunt your powers in a space where mortals could witness it. You weren't even aware of your surroundings." Ebonee Johnson, the leader of the Crystal Coast coven I'd recently joined, towered over me with a disapproving glare.

"It was just a few of us making sure everything was perfect for the reception," I exclaimed, upset that my voice wavered with nerves. "I didn't expect anyone to sneak up on us."

Instead of scolding me more, she stood in silent disapproval until I uttered a quiet apology. Her haughty habit of exacting her power at all the wrong times continued to be a thorn in my side. I searched the area for my friends to back me up and noticed other members of the coven walking around the perimeter with their hands up, clearly spellcasting.

"Wait, aren't they also *flaunting their powers?*" I asked with a little too much sass in my tone.

Ebonee brushed her long braids off her shoulder. "Unlike you, I positioned someone at the entrance to make sure we wouldn't be disturbed. And not that I need to explain myself to you, but they're making sure the party will not be ruined by bugs or mosquitoes."

Although I wanted to push back and argue against the hypocrisy, I appreciated the attempt to make our night bite free. "Any chance you can throw in something to keep the temperature and humidity perfect?"

The coven leader shook her head in dismissal. "If you had stayed after the binding ceremony like you were supposed to instead of taking off with your friends, you might have been included in talks about what we would and would not do. As it is, yes, some basic pleasant weather spells have already been spellcast at the behest of the bride's parents."

"They actually wanted to do something positive for the wedding? That's…" I trailed off, trying to come up with a more polite finish than *surprising*. "Good. I'm glad they didn't ask you to find some sort of coven by-laws to prevent the union altogether."

Ebonee shifted on her feet and glanced away for a moment before reinstating her authority with crossed arms. "What I do or don't talk about with other coven members is my business and strictly confidential. The same benefit would extend to you if you ever really committed to becoming a true participant. I'm beginning to think allowing you and your friends inside our circle might not have been the best decision. Having a Jewell in our organization hasn't been as beneficial as I'd once hoped."

My jaw dropped at such a sudden turn in the conversation, but before I could spout off my list of grievances that had been growing since my first day in the coven, Luke approached us and stood by my side, his arm snaking around my waist.

"Excuse me, ladies," he interrupted, waiting with vampiric patience for Ebonee to acknowledge his presence. "Members of the band would like to get to the stage to do a final sound check, but they aren't being let into the area."

"Exactly how did you get by my people?" Ebonee huffed, a load of judgment radiating off her in waves.

Showing off his perfect teeth in a wide grin, Luke answered, "Oh, I've been told I can be pretty charming. Right, honey?" His fingers dug into my hip with purpose, and he pulled me closer and brushed his lips against my temple. Despite the situation at hand, my cheeks heated a little.

The overt display of affection irritated the coven leader to her limits. "Fine. I'll take care of things." She stomped off and left the two of us alone.

I pushed Luke off with a playful shove. "You are terrible."

He wiggled his eyebrows at me. "Terribly charming, you mean." Before I could retort with a snarky remark, he planted his lips on mine and kissed me silly.

A squeal of feedback from the speakers reverberated in the air and interrupted our romantic moment. "Let the woman breathe, man," a voice teased through a microphone.

My giggling response broke the romantic moment. "Hey, Hunter," I called out to the lead singer of the band that Harrison had hired for their event.

"Hey, Ruby Mae Jewell, get over here." He gestured for me to approach the stage. "Me and the boys got a favor to ask you."

I nodded and took one step only to be held back with a light tug on my hand. Luke pressed my back to his front and kissed the sensitive spot on my neck, his hot breath tickling my ear. "They better not be asking for a dance tonight. Your card is full."

A tingle of excitement raced through my veins. "Don't worry. I didn't wear this dress for anyone but you." Squeezing his hand, I let go and added a little extra sass in my sashay for him to enjoy.

Hunter Ford and the rest of Tailgate Down were regular musicians at the Tiki during the summer tourist months when we'd opened the patio and doubled our monetary income every time they were booked. I greeted EJ and Mac with quick hugs and waved at Hart, their terrific drummer sitting behind his kit.

"Hey, Rue, where's my hug?" Hunter set his acoustic guitar on a stand and held his arms out wide.

"Where's my twenty bucks?" I shot back at him.

His eyes widened. "What are you talking about?"

I placed a hand on my hip. "Remember the bet I made with you? That Harrison would be the one to go home with that honey blonde thing that night y'all played at the Tiki and *not* you?"

His mouth formed a small *O* as he recalled the situation. "Well, he was a major player back in the day. But I gotta tell you, I'm glad to see him settling down. Gives all of us bad boys hope that one day we might be tamed."

"Hey, I resemble that remark." EJ played a few power chords before giving the bass player, Levi, heck for being late to the set up.

Hunter ignored his bandmates and got down to business. "About that favor."

I snapped my fingers and stuck my palm out. "Twenty bucks first."

He groaned in mock annoyance and pulled his wallet out of his back pocket, slapping the money in my hand. "Here. Now, can you stop busting my chops and listen to my request?"

"Sure. What's up?" I asked.

"Well, Harrison and Azalea requested *Until I Loved You* as their first dance together. Remember that time you sang with us?" His face morphed into an expression of innocent appeal while he batted big puppy dog eyes at me.

Nervous butterflies took wing in my stomach. "I was tipsy and being dared by all my friends. No way. I can't sing with y'all," I insisted.

EJ, too nosy for his own good, joined the conversation. "Of course you can. You've got an incredible voice."

I waved my hands in front of me. "No, you don't get it. I mean, yes, I sing at karaoke night for fun."

"Then sing tonight for fun. And for the bride and groom. You'll be fine. But they've asked for us to add an extra verse at the end." Mac, the keyboardist, handed me a sheet with the words of the song written down.

Hunter picked up his guitar and strummed the intro to the song, ignoring my pleas. Without stopping, he launched into the first verse, raising his eyebrows when it was my turn to sing. Still sure the idea of me singing with them might be disastrous, I clutched the paper in my trembling fingers and joined in. The first notes were a little shaky, but as I got into the song and realized the beautiful significance of the lyrics, the desire to be a part of the important moment for Azalea and Harrison chased away the butterflies.

Mac listened and stopped us a couple of times, making suggestions of adjustments to our harmonies or who should sing where. After a couple of run throughs, the first guests filtered into the space, so we had to stop.

"Promise me, if you think I won't do it justice," I pleaded, "then don't call me up on stage."

"Girl, you'll be great. Harrison and Azalea will be surprised and pleased," Hunter insisted. "Now, go join your boyfriend before he gets the wrong idea that I'm trying to hit on you. Oh, and if you need a little extra courage, bourbon or scotch always works for me."

"Good advice." With careful steps, I made my way off the stage and joined Luke to update him and get his help and reassurance in my singing abilities.

With the timing perfect, the sun was setting and casting orange and red hues over the waters of the Bogue Sound behind the venue. Some of the professional photographer's team circulated around, taking pictures of the gorgeous event space and guests enjoying themselves. Waiters passed by with trays of tonight's signature cocktail of spiked sweet tea with lemonade mojitos while shiny buckets filled with ice and champagne bottles were placed at every table for future toasts.

Two buffet tables full of comfort food appetizers opened, and my friends and I filled plates with fried chicken sliders and tangy coleslaw, individual servings of shrimp and grits, local oysters with muscadine mignonette, pimento cheese and bacon crostini, and deviled eggs.

"You'll ruin your dinner if you eat all that," Dani accused.

To shut her up, I held up a deviled egg in front of her mouth until she opened wide and ate the whole thing in one bite. "I gotta do something to distract my nerves and soak up the alcohol from the mojitos. I think I drank down that first one a little too fast."

Dani demanded to know why I was nervous, and she summoned the rest of our group to join us. I cringed at the suggestion of me singing the song for the first dance, but they all encouraged me with enthusiastic reassurances.

Cate clapped with glee. "You'll be perfect. Turns out the lead singer is smart *and* sexy." She stood on her tiptoes to see over the crowd and catch a glimpse of Hunter.

"If you don't mind hooking up with a bit of a player, I can introduce you at the end of the festivities," I offered, hiding my face behind my hands and wishing for my embarrassment to recede.

The quiet music in the background stopped when Mac played a jingling chord on the keyboard.

Hunter instructed us to ready our glasses as he announced the arrival of the wedding party. He introduced everyone and waited for the party to line up and make a tunnel for the bride and groom.

"Y'all lift your glasses in honor of Azalea and Harrison Dobbs," Hunter shouted.

We toasted them and took sips. Someone clinked a knife against the glass until everyone joined in, forcing the newlyweds to kiss. The guests took their places at their designated tables, and we watched the groom accept a shovel and a microphone from one of the groomsmen before speaking.

"Thank you for being here with us tonight. I look around and am feeling blessed to be surrounded by those who love us and wish us well." He paused to accept the applause and random whoops of delight.

Crystal leaned back in her chair to whisper to me. "Bet that was meant for her parents."

"Mm-hmm," I agreed, proud to see Harrison stand up for what was his.

The groom held up the shovel. "Some of you may not be aware of the Southern tradition of burying a bottle of bourbon. The story goes that if we buried it upside down before the wedding on an evening that matched the weather we wanted for tonight, we'd be sure to lock in beautiful weather for our reception."

He nodded his chin at the last colorful rays of the sun setting over the water. "I'd say it's time to dig up that bottle and celebrate the success of holding onto tradition and giving my bride the perfect night."

Hunter and his band played background music while Harrison went to dig under a nearby magnolia tree. The groom held up the bottle covered in dirt, and servers placed bottles of bourbon and clean tumblers on all the tables.

Once he opened the dirty-covered bottle and shared with the main wedding party, he lifted his glass. "To my wife." His lips spread into a beaming smile while he gazed at her with burning adoration. "Azalea, I never knew love until I loved you."

I gasped, recognizing the words from the chorus of the song I was supposed to sing. Grabbing a tumbler, I tossed down the bourbon, coughing at the immediate heat of the drink at the back of my throat. Luke patted my back with an amused twinkle in his eyes.

Whether it was the drinks or my friends surrounding me, I settled into enjoying the rest of the reception as best I could. The incredible wait staff place plates of the main course in front of us at the same time, and I appreciated the meticulous presentation of unpretentious food. Most of my friends at the table gobbled down the generous portion of pulled pork with Eastern North Carolina vinegar sauce, sopping both up with crumbling cornbread. Although my plate was loaded with food I loved, the upcoming song and dance occupied my mind as the moment drew closer and closer. When servers whisked away the empty dishes, I'd barely finished half.

The soft music Tailgate Down had provided during the meal stopped, and Gloria's brother and best man Wesley stood up with a microphone in his hand.

My stomach clenched, knowing that the dance would come after the toasts. While everyone else listened, laughed, and got emotional over stories that revealed more about Azalea and Harrison and their journey to tonight, I found the wrinkled paper with the lyrics and went over them in a panic.

Luke scooted my chair closer to him and rubbed my tense neck with his strong hands. "You'll be fine, *cara*." He kissed the top of my head.

The microphone got passed down the line of the wedding party until it reached Azalea's parents. Her father glared at it, and I feared he would refuse to take it and toast his daughter and her new husband. The weighted hush of everyone waiting expanded into long seconds of tense silence with a few whispers here and there. Closing his eyes with a sigh, Azalea's dad accepted the microphone.

He reached his hand out for his wife and took a deep breath. "We thank y'all for coming and supporting our daughter on her special day. Azalea, your mother and I would like you to know that, just like when you were little, we will always be here for you. Through the good and the bad. No matter what happens in your future, you will always have us. We love you."

Rage obliterated my nerves, and I stormed my way around the tables full of stunned guests to the stage. Hunter offered his hand to help me up the stairs. "Wow. Harrison wasn't kidding when he said Azalea's parents didn't like him."

"Yeah, I don't think any of us knew how bad it was. They've both been hiding it. I guess they wanted to try and deal with it on their own." I regretted not knowing the truth of their struggle so maybe I could have done more than just get her drunk the night before her wedding.

"Well, how about you help us out in making the newlyweds feel a little better." Hunter winked at me and held up his finger, asking me to wait on the side. He walked to the center of the stage and took command. "Thank you to everyone for your kind words in support of this wonderful couple in their future together. And now, we'd like to invite them to the middle of the floor for their first dance together as Mr. and Mrs. Dobbs.

The crowd brightened and cheered, happy for the couple but also probably relieved for the awkward moment to pass. I pressed my hand against my middle, trying to keep those butterflies contained again.

Hunter waited for Azalea and Harrison to take their place and give him the signal they were ready. When he had their attention, the lead singer indicated for me to join him at the front with a tip of his head. With hesitant steps, I did my best to ignore the immense pressure of being watched. When I arrived at center stage, I attempted to smile and look out at the audience but managed a weird grimace.

Holy hexes, so many people had turned their attention on me, waiting! My knees knocked together underneath the skirt of my pretty dress.

Hunter covered his mic and leaned in my direction. "Close your eyes, take a deep breath, and let it out. Then when you're ready, focus on the look on the bride and groom's face. I've got the first verse like we've rehearsed. You'll do great, Rue."

His acoustic guitar picked the intro of the song, and the rest of the band came in with flawless precision. After one more deep breath, I opened my eyes and found Azalea elated and euphoric being held tight in Harrison's arms as they began their first steps of the traditional dance. My friend and former co-worker mouthed a thanks over his wife's head, and Azalea gave me a quick thumbs up.

Hunter got closer to finishing the first verse, and I steadied myself to join him in the chorus. Grasping the mic with both hands, I gathered my courage and sang with absolute conviction to the words.

> You are everything I wanted
> And more than I deserve
> You have filled the empty spaces of my
>   heart
> And now that I have found you
> We will never be apart
> From all that I have learned,
> this much is true
> I didn't know love until
> I loved you

By the time we got through the second verse, another round of the chorus, and the bridge, there was barely a dry eye in the entire place. Hunter nodded at me when we sang the duet for the special verse added just for tonight.

> Now, here it's our wedding day
> My heart is so full
> There's just so much I need to say
> I promise you I'll try to honor
> All our wedding vows
> Through good and through bad
> I'm gonna love you
> More than I do now

When I repeated the chorus, my heart soared in the moment and with celebration of the meaning of the lyrics. I sought out Luke while the song came to a close and sang right to him, hoping he could hear my devotion for him with the final notes.

Harrison twirled Azalea away from him and back, finishing their dance with a careful dip. All of the guests erupted into applause and hollers as he planted a dramatic kiss before pulling her upright. She stumbled into his arms in a heap of laughter and tears.

Hopped up on adrenaline, I couldn't stop smiling. My friends hooted a little too loudly when Hunter thanked me for joining in. With a shy wave to the crowd, I hurried to the side of the stage and let the professionals take over.

Luke met me and escorted me back onto solid ground. Grabbing my hand, he dragged me away from the lit area of the reception to a darker, more secluded spot behind a nearby tree.

"What are you doing?" I asked with a giggle, pleased to have my boyfriend no longer holding back.

He stopped and yanked me into a tight embrace. "I needed a moment alone with my girlfriend to show her how amazing she is, and that I felt every single word of that song."

He placed a knuckle under my chin and tipped my head up. His eyes blazed with feral desire, and I wondered if he would attempt to ravish me right here, right now. Instead of crashing his lips against mine, he sighed and brushed a finger down my cheek. Taking the lead, he rocked me back and forth in our own private slow dance, never taking his eyes off mine.

When the music for the other official wedding dances stopped, so did he. Luke stepped back and ran his hand through his hair. "Listen, Rue, I'm aware I've been a little distant with you lately."

His bringing up a sadder topic doused my excitement. I placed a finger over his lips keep him from following it up with anything that would ruin our night. "Good, because you have. But we can talk about all that later. For now, escort me back and dance with me until my feet fall off, please."

He tilted his head and observed me with interested eyes as if he wasn't quite sure what to do. Kissing each fingertip, he gave in and linked his fingers through mine. We sauntered out of the shadows in the direction of the rest of my friends as they flooded the dance floor, kicking up a storm to Tailgate Down's cover of a popular country hit.

Ms. Robin intercepted us right before we got to our table, giving me a warm hug. "I wanted to tell you before I headed home to rest that I think you have the most marvelous voice."

"Thank you so much for the compliment. I swear, half of my even being able to get up there was knowing I looked like I do in your dress," I countered. "Did you and Tara have a good day? I haven't seen her around."

"Oh, she stayed for the beginnings of the reception but said she wasn't feeling well." The designer frowned until she glanced at my attire again. The sight of it brought a smile back to her face. "And that dress isn't mine, dear. It's yours. In my shop, it's just a bunch of fabric, but you've brought it to life tonight."

Luke reached his hand out and captured the designer's, bringing it to his lips and kissing the back of it in reverence. "Thank you for your talents."

Ms. Robin cheeks reddened. "Oh my but aren't you the charming one." She fanned herself with her free hand. "Ruby Mae, I hope you'll be visiting me again much sooner than you think." With a wink to both of us, she left.

Tipsy on sweet tea and lemonade mojitos, the chance to sing for the newlyweds, and the hope for me and Luke, the rest of the night passed in a blur. We danced to almost every single song until we'd worked off every extra calorie from the meal. Luke and I got in at least two more slow dances together, and I marveled at his skills in leading me around the dance floor better than a ballroom professional.

When it came time for the bouquet toss, I took my place in the middle of the floor with the rest of the giddy girls. Azalea counted down, and by the time she got to *one*, everyone around me stepped out of the way. The sneaky bride turned to face us and lobbed the flowers right at me.

Worried that the heat of my embarrassment

might ignite the bouquet, I chastised my friends for setting me up and searched for Luke, fearing his disapproval. Instead, he laughed and held up a tumbler of scotch to toast me. Odie clapped an arm over his shoulder, no doubt giving him heck over having to marry me sometime in the future.

During the cake cutting, I expected someone to get a face full of frosting. But Azalea and Harrison fed each other without making a mess. The efficient servers appeared at the tables, bringing pre-cut slices of the red velvet cake with elaborate buttercream frosting decorations to everyone. A buffet table of other Southern sweets opened up, and we splurged on fancy banana pudding, pecan pie, and peach cobbler. Knowing we'd work off the calories with more dancing, we indulged our sugar cravings.

Some of the older guests left after the last scheduled activity, including Azalea's parents. But a lot of us stayed on the dance floor, getting our groove on to every song Hunter and his band could throw at us. They started taking requests, and we tried to trip them up with more than just country tunes. The only surprise came when Hunter belted out *Shoulda Known Better* by a popular female country star. Why he would agree to sing a song about a cheater, I'd never know, but the tune was so catchy that we shook more than just our tail feathers until we were breathless.

"I gotta hit the Ladies' room," I announced, hoping to head toward the facilities before the band played another good song.

As if sensing my predicament and picking the perfect time to mess with me, EJ tore through the familiar electric guitar intro to a fun country party anthem.

Cate grabbed my hand. "Come on," she whined. "One more song."

"I gotta go," I insisted, pulling out of her grasp. "I promise I'll be right back."

A little lightheaded from all the merriment, I stumbled my way to the guest bathrooms inside the house, thankful for a moment's peace to sort myself out and make myself a little more presentable. I admired the gorgeous dress and what it did for me in the full-length mirror before heading back toward the twinkling lights and laughter of the reception.

With careful steps, I walked down the dimly lit path from the house back to the party. Recognizing the distinctive cackling of my friends, I sped up to find out what the joke was. As I approached the edge of the activities, a strange sound off to my left caught my ear. Something about it felt out of place, and I stood still and strained to hear it again.

Staring into the wooded area right behind the wedding party table, I tried to make out what might have made the noise. Light filtered in patches but didn't illuminate enough of the landscape for me to identify an animal or anything recognizable. Hunter's voice announced they would be playing their last song, and I shrugged, figuring my fuzzy brain from all the drinking and having fun had imagined it.

The band played the first few bars until a sudden shriek in the air interrupted them. Chills broke out over my skin, and I stumbled and struggled forward to where the scream had come from.

"What's going on?" I asked, approaching a darkened shadow of a figure. "What happened?"

"Help! You have to help me!" The bride's high-pitched panic pierced the darkness.

Without a thought as to who might catch me, I spellcast a small ball of light. The glow reflected on not one but two people, and I held my hand over my mouth to contain a scream.

Azalea knelt over a crumpled man in a tuxedo, both hands wrapped around the hilt of a knife buried into his back.

CHAPTER FOUR

"What are you doing?" I yelled at the bride, fear and alarm burning off the rest of my buzz.

Without hesitation, I lunged at her, struggling to yank her off of whoever was lying on the ground. We tussled enough that we jostled the body, and the figure groaned in pain.

Azalea attempted to fight me off. "Don't!" she grunted. "I have to get it out of him!" With more strength than I anticipated, she pushed me backwards onto my behind. "Somebody did this to him, and I have to fix it."

Her words sunk into my head, and their meaning dawned on me. I scrambled to my knees to stop her.

"Wait!" I demanded, placing my hands over hers again to keep her from making a huge mistake. "If you're trying to take the knife out, don't." Using all my reserves, I ignored the pain of her boney elbows in my ribs and pried her fingers off the hilt of the knife.

"You're. Hurting. Him. Ow! And me," she accused, cradling the hand I peeled off.

I gritted my teeth. "Then stop fighting me and listen. Whoever this is, you could do way more damage than what's already been done if you pull the blade out."

With a gasp, she let go and held up both hands in surrender. Looking at me for the first time with widened eyes, her breath came in pants while she rambled. "I…wasn't thinking. It's just, Harrison and I had talked about sneaking off to steal a couple of minutes alone. When I couldn't find him on the dance floor, I thought this was some sort of fun game and we could, you know, make out or something as husband and wife while everyone was having fun. And then I got worried when he didn't answer his phone, so I went searching around until I almost stumbled over him here. As soon as I knew it was him, I freaked out, especially when I saw the knife. And it's hurting him, and I'm the one who's supposed to take care of him." She drew in a shaky breath. "I'm his wife."

Placing a hand on her trembling shoulder, I spoke in a deliberate, calm tone, "Trust me, pulling out that knife is going to be the opposite of fixing it. I need you to breathe, Azalea, while I see how bad it is."

It took great effort on my part not to freak out as much as the bride was, but the last thing we needed was for her to lose her mind and pull out that knife. Gathering as much courage as I could, I crawled forward to check out the body of my friend.

"Harrison." I tapped on his shoulder. "Can you hear me?" With a little more effort, I shook him, hoping he would at least grunt again, but he made no reply. Fear gnawed at my gut and I froze, not knowing what else to do.

"What's going on here?" Luke's deep voice interrupted us, and I yelped, losing control of the light ball and plunging us back into the dark. He sniffed the air. "Why do I smell blood?" He flashed to my side with vampiric speed and grasped my hands, scenting them. "This isn't yours."

I hadn't even notice that Azalea transferred some of the blood from her hands to mine. Although I couldn't see the crimson liquid on either of us without creating another light orb, I didn't want it on me. Luke pulled the pocket square out of his suit jacket and wiped my hands clean.

Azalea crumpled forward with a sob, and I caught her, letting her bawl on my shoulder. With sympathy and pity, I held onto her despite my desire to figure out what was going on with the body. "I can't see anything anymore, but I think that's Harrison lying behind us. There's a knife sticking out his back on the left side, and I think he might be…" I couldn't bring myself to add *dead*.

"He isn't," Luke said, responding to my unspoken word. "I can see much more than you can, and he's definitely still alive. Although we need to get him medical attention right away. He's having a hard time breathing."

Hope caused the bride to lose the rest of her control, and she wailed in both distress and relief, dragging herself back to her new husband's side. "Harrison, I'm here." She gripped his hand with both of hers. "I'm right beside you."

Luke advised her not to move the body. After he settled her next to her husband, he helped me to my feet. "Did you see what happened? Did Azalea do that?"

I shook my head. "I wish I knew. I didn't see anything. All I heard was her crying before I discovered her hovering over Harrison's body. Even though she's not making a lot of sense, I think she found him that way and thought she should pull the knife out. I stopped her because I figured it would make him bleed out or something."

"It very well could have. You did good." He kissed my temple. "But now you need to do the right thing. Call 9-1-1 to get the paramedics and the authorities here. At this point, it's a crime scene and you're a witness."

"But a witness to what? I mean, I don't understand what's going on." The only thing I knew for certain was that whoever had done this to Harrison on his wedding night was a hateful, awful person.

"Nobody knows right now, but that's not your job to figure out. Follow protocol. Call the police. And after that, you know the next step, right?" he prodded, squatting down next to Azalea whose blubbering was getting out of control again from her shock.

I wrinkled my nose at the inevitable. "I have to call Ebonee and inform her because a coven member is involved." Blowing out a long breath, I fumbled in the shadows to find my dropped clutch. With the beaded bag in my grasp, I pulled out the spell phone. "This night just took a turn none of us could have expected."

It didn't take long for others to follow the commotion and find our tableau of horror. The rest of the guests crowded around the edges until the paramedics arrived with the police. Based on what Ebonee advised me, I understood the importance of cooperating with the officer in charge in order to get through the ordeal and allow her time to alert the local wardens and her magical law enforcement contacts. With the Wallace House located on a spit of land between Cedar Point and Bogue right on the water, I couldn't predict who had jurisdiction.

Since good news travels fast and bad news travels faster, a lot of attention focused on me with the speculation that I knew more than I actually did. Even my friends didn't totally believe me when I said I didn't know anything other than Harrison was hurt and Azalea had found him. A teeny tiny part of me questioned whether or not she might have done the deed herself, but I chased away those niggling demons after watching her weeping and wailing over him while the paramedics rolled the gurney onto the lit pathway back to the parking lot. Gloria stayed by her best friend's side, her face pale and strained.

"I feel so bad for them," Dani stated, wiping a tear from her cheek.

Cate hugged her from the side. "I know. Everything had been so beautiful, too."

I checked around the area near us. "Where's Crystal?"

My cousin waved at Gloria, who glanced back at us with the saddest eyes. "Odie stole her off the dance floor about the time you left to go to the bathroom. I don't want to think about why they left in such a hurry. Guess it's a good thing they missed all this."

Luke stayed by my left side but remained so still, it unnerved me. "You okay?" I asked.

He grunted in affirmation. "I don't like that you'll be dragged into this."

I attempted to ease his tension by sliding my arm around his middle and forcing him to put his around my shoulders to cuddle me. His body felt more like a boulder than a pillow. "Honey, they're my friends. You know I would have gotten involved whether I'd found them or not. And remember, if I hadn't stopped Azalea, Harrison might have been in bigger trouble. Now, he has a chance."

"His pulse was weakened," admitted Luke. "Based on how he was laying on his side, I'd guess the knife got him in the spleen. Or maybe the kidney. Neither one is good. And if there's internal bleeding…"

"Holy hexes," I muttered. "You sure?"

His eyes found mine, and I shivered under his gaze. "I'm more than well acquainted with the components of the body. I'm sure."

My instincts forced me to take a step away from him, but he shook himself out of his melancholy and pulled me back into a protective embrace. Kissing the top of my head, he attempted to act indifferent. I chose not to give his charade away to my friends.

Hunter and the rest of the band approached me after the medics disappeared and the wail of the ambulance's siren rose in the air like a mournful tune. I made quick introductions of my friends to the band.

The lead singer scratched the back of his neck. "Man, I hope he pulls through. It's a heck of a thing to happen, and on their wedding night."

Since we'd been instructed not to go anywhere until the local authorities figured out how to handle breaking down the scene and talking to us, I eased some of my nerves and fed my curiosity. "Hunt, did any of y'all see anything strange from your view-point on the stage?"

EJ snorted. "Other than spotting some sneaky old lady put some of the utensils in her purse at one point, no."

"We were all kinda busy," Mac defended. He rolled his shoulders and sighed. "Sorry. That came out a little harsher than I meant it."

I waved him off. "It's okay. We've been through a lot and are a little touchy right now. Rightfully so." Without a timeline of how long we'd be required to stick around, none of us knew what to expect. Uncertainty kept us unsettled.

A commotion at the far end of the crowd caught my attention, and I stretched on my tiptoes to see who was addressing people in such a stern tone. My stomach dropped when I spotted Deputy Sheriff Marshall Caine moving the bystanders out of the way.

"Please step to the side, thank you," he said while moving through the throng. "We will be conducting interviews here shortly, so do not leave until you've been cleared to do so."

"Sheriff Caine, would it be possible for us to sit down while we wait?" I asked. Agreement from others rose in chorus with my request.

The county law enforcement officer twitched his mustache in agitation when he recognized me. "I'm sure our team will get through our questions for each of you as fast as we can. Demanding that we go faster won't get the job done."

"That's not what she asked, Deputy Sheriff," countered Luke. "She asked if we could gather the chairs and sit down while we wait. Surely that won't break any official protocol."

Caine licked his fingertip and turned pages in his notepad. "And your name is?"

My boyfriend stood to his full height, an air of authority settling over him. "Luke." He paused, allowing the sheriff to write it down but also forcing the man to wait for him to speak. "My surname is Manson." He spelled it out with slow deliberation.

"And your reason for being here tonight?" Deputy Caine interrogated.

Luke smirked. "To attend the wedding of my girl-friend's friends."

"And please identify both by name and by indication who said girlfriend is," the officer insisted, ignoring my presence at Luke's side.

I rolled my eyes. "At the rate you're going, we'll be here for another couple of days. We won't need chairs, we'll need tents." I waved my hand in the air.

"Me. I'm his girlfriend. And my name is Jewell. Ruby Mae Jewell. That's spelled R-U-B—"

"I know how to spell your name, Miss Jewell," he interrupted, a terse frown forming underneath his mustache. "I'm more than acquainted with it from our previous encounters. Plus, I have a note here that you might be a key witness."

"Good, then you'll know that I'm also not one for waiting around. Can you tell us exactly how long this is going to take and what we should expect?" I demanded, crossing my arms and forgetting that by doing so, it highlighted my exposed cleavage.

The sheriff's eyes dipped to my chest for a brief second. He cleared his throat and regained his composure. "It'll take as long as it takes." He turned on his uniformed heel to walk away.

"Hey, aren't you going to interview me now?" I called after him.

He waved his pen in the air. "I'll get to you eventually. In the meantime, yes."

I huffed with impatience at his petty attempt to control me. "Yes, what?"

"Yes, you can sit in chairs while you wait." He joined other law enforcement personnel and conferred with them, pointing back at me once or twice. Whatever he told them, it probably wasn't all that positive.

Luke helped to drag chairs over for others to sit on although he chose to pace nearby rather than to join me and my friends. Hunter scooted his chair right next to mine. "Okay, spill it. Who's the unpleasant guy with the 'stache?"

Dani, Cate, and I gave an abbreviated version of the murder investigation that had happened on my family's land, leaving out the part about the magical crystal ball at the root of it all. However, we held nothing back about our general dislike for the sheriff's insistence of my uncle's guilt and lack of apology when Dani's father was found innocent.

Levi, the quiet bassist, surprised us with his utterance of conviction. "He sounds like an absolute tool."

"He speaks," joked EJ, punching his bandmate's arm.

"Well, I don't like watching those with authority abuse their power." Levi sat back in his chair with his arms crossed over his chest, pursing his lips.

We fell into quiet banter while waiting for our turn to come. While the rest of the officers spread out to get as many interviews done as possible, nobody approached us. The occasional smirks from

Caine confirmed my suspicion that he'd arranged a little power play and prevented anyone from talking to me or my friends.

When only our small group remained, I stood up. "Finally."

"You can sit back down, Ms. Jewell, and wait your turn," Sheriff Caine instructed.

"I don't think so, Deputy. Ms. Jewell will be talking with me." A new woman in khakis, a simple white button-down blouse, and a suit jacket approached the last officers surrounding our group with a purposeful stride. "The rest of you need to make sure you've recorded what you can of the crime scene, and let's be finished for the night. I want to see the reports on my desk in the morning."

Several of the officers who had been helping Caine in his delay scattered with the commands of the newcomer. The sheriff glared at the woman. "I'm sure everything will be in order, Lieutenant. I've made sure of that."

"Glad to hear that, Deputy. I wouldn't want someone who was looking to move up in the department making things harder than they needed to be." She gestured at the rest of us staring back at her with mouths agape. "I'm sure if I interviewed these people myself, all of them would speak to your efficient handling of the situation, yes?"

Caine replied with a solitary sniff. "I'll make sure to finish the last interviews right away."

"Good." The lieutenant snapped her fingers twice at me. "Ms. Jewell, please accompany me." Without waiting for me to stand, she marched in the direction of where Harrison's injured body had been found. Some of the officers still cataloguing the scene scrambled to finish and get out of her way without her needing to ask them to move.

Once she cleared the immediate area, she pulled her suit jacket open and showed me a badge hanging from the inside of the lining. "My name is Olivia Alwin, and I'm a lieutenant with the county sheriff's office as well as the regional warden's division. I came as soon as Ebonee Johnson, head of the Crystal Coast Coven, alerted me. I understand you might have more information on what happened here." She stopped flashing me her badge and pulled out a notebook.

Not often did I find myself without anything to say. I stammered and struggled to gain control of my words, speechless from shock and awe at the lieutenant's commanding presence. Coughing once to regain composure, I explained to her exactly what I'd observed.

"So, you didn't see who wielded the knife?" she clarified.

I repeated the same answer I'd given to everyone else. "No. Only that Azalea was touching it when I arrived, and I felt I needed to stop her." Hearing the words come out of my mouth, I realized the immediate conclusion I would come to if I heard them. "I was trying to keep her from pulling the knife out."

Watching the lieutenant write down my account, I cringed. Everything was coming out wrong.

"I mean, I don't think she was doing anything other than panicking and not in her right mind at the time." Nope, that wasn't much better. "So, she thought she might be able to save him, but extracting the knife would have hurt him more."

"Or killed him on the spot," Lieutenant Alwin stated, glancing up at me. "You did good stopping her from causing more damage."

"But I'm failing at trying to tell you I don't think Azalea was the one who hurt Harrison. I believe her when she says she found him already stabbed." Having finally gotten to my point, I tried to peek to make sure she wrote that down.

"Hmm."

The lieutenant's enigmatic reply worried me, but I didn't want to prolong our talk in case I fumbled my words and messed things up even more. She walked me back to where Luke waited for me, the last guest still present other than me. Relief swept through me, and for the first time tonight, exhaustion replaced the adrenaline. Still, I wouldn't be able to sleep tonight thinking I'd wrongly implicated a friend.

Lieutenant Alwin collected my contact information in her notebook and closed it, but I refused to quit. "Listen, I want to make it perfectly clear. There's no way I would ever believe Azalea did this. You should be making a list of possible suspects or whatever it is you do to figure out who to investigate."

She placed her notebook back in its place in her suit pocket. "I'm sure you're recalling your bad experience with how your uncle was wrongfully accused of the murder on your family's property. Let me inform you that I work from evidence. I'll let the facts talk to me and not allow speculations or assumptions to drive my conclusions. Is that clear, Ms. Jewell?"

Although her tone held a slight chill, her words comforted me. "Clear and welcomed, Lieutenant."

She nodded once in dismissal, and I spied a small hint of a satisfied grin. Once back with my group, Luke offered me the crook of his arm and escorted me to the parking lot. We passed Caine on our way, and I dared to wiggle my fingers in a cheeky farewell, feeling a little more secure that this time, things might go right.

CHAPTER FIVE

My dead-but-not-departed great-grandmother popped my knuckles with her spatula. "Stop trying to steal bacon out of the skillet. Those are for your guest."

"For my *mortal* guests, which means it's supposed to look like I made breakfast. Not some ghost. And what cook in their right mind doesn't steal bacon while they're frying it up? I'm going for authenticity here, Granny," I defended, finishing the strip I'd snatched. Totally worth the sting on the back of my hand.

Dani entered the kitchen. "Table's all set, and Mom brought over a bunch of baked goods from the cafe already."

A timer dinged, and Granny Jo threw a pair of

oven mitts at me. "That'll be the buttermilk biscuits to go with the country ham and jelly. Better get a move on because if you burn my biscuits, I'll haunt you every day of your life."

I rolled my eyes, obeying and removing the cast iron skillet loaded with golden brown biscuits from the oven. "Not much of a threat when you already do that."

My ghostly great-grandmother wiggled her eyebrows. "Ah, but I'll burn your little cottage down and force you to move in here with me and all the other family spirits," she threatened in a dramatic wavering voice. "Now, put in that breakfast casserole dish and set the timer for twenty minutes."

The thought of having to live one night in the family homestead shut me right up. Sure, it appeared as a normal white farmhouse on the outside, but because of my family's extensive magical ancestry, the house grew and adjusted to accommodate all the Jewell family members, alive or dead.

"Yes, ma'am," I promptly replied with a tiny salute.

My cousin ridiculed the two of us, ignoring our familial snark back and forth and taking dishes out to the dining room table.

"I know you told your daddy and your uncle

everything that happened last night before they took off, but remind me who's coming to our house this morning?" Granny Jo asked, frying up some sizzling hash browns in another skillet.

"They're members of a country band that used to play at the bar I worked at," I explained. "I convinced them to stop by here before they headed back home to Virginia. I've got something I want to ask them about last night."

As tired as I was after getting home, my mind kept me awake for a few more hours mulling over every detail. About the time I'd begin to drift off to sleep, I'd recall the sight of Azalea bent over Harrison's limp body. This morning, I was feeling almost too weak to whip a gnat. My need to gain a little energy to get through the meal definitely warranted at least one more piece of stolen bacon.

"They're here," Dani announced from the foyer.

I tied an apron around my middle. "Okay, you gotta make yourself scarce."

Granny Jo pouted and hovered in the air. "But I wanna see them. I thought you told me they were something to look at."

"So, you were listening to me," I accused. Voices got closer to the kitchen, and I heard Dani speak loud enough to give us a warning we might be having visitors. "Come on, Granny. If you're not gonna go away, then at least disappear. Otherwise, we'll have a whole different kettle of fish to fry, trying to explain your see-through presence." Snatching the spatula from her, I shooed her away like an errant fly.

"And this is the kitchen." Dani popped her head around the corner to make sure the coast was clear for her to let them in.

"Mornin', boys." I waved the kitchen utensil at the bandmates. "If y'all are hungry, we've already got stuff set out in the dining room."

"You don't have to tell me twice." EJ pushed his friends out of the way and fought with Hart to make it to the table first. Levi shook his head at their shenanigans but followed in companionable silence.

"Can we help you carry anything out?" Hunter picked up the piled plate of biscuits. "Here, I'll take this to the table."

"I can help you finish up in here," Mac offered once we were alone. "I've been told I know my way around a stove."

A slight sigh sounded in my ear, and my great-grandmother's approval of the young man gave me a serious case of the heebie jeebies. "These hash browns are the last dish other than the casserole in the oven." I flipped the pan over, dumping the crispy potato dish on the plate.

"Then before we leave, we'll help out with the dishes. If you cook, we'll clean," he promised.

As soon as he left the room, Granny Jo clapped her hands behind me, causing me to leap out of my skin. "Ooh, a man who can cook *and* clean. Sign me up, buttercup."

"Ew, Granny, they're all way too young for you. Like, centuries too young." I'd have to take a hot poker to my eyes to kill the mental picture of my departed great-grandmother getting all moony-eyed over my friends.

"Hey, just because I'm dead doesn't mean I'm actually *dead*. I can appreciate good looking men when I see them. And boy, I'm gonna want to see them." The timer dinged again. "You'd better take that sausage and egg casserole to the table with some pep in your step or I'll do it myself. Might be worth scaring the actual pants off of those boys."

Not caring if I dropped the piping hot dish, I almost sprinted to the dining room to get as much distance as possible between me and my kinky spectral kin.

Cate and Crystal let themselves into the house and joined in the easy conversation. It did not slip my notice that Cate positioned herself right next to Hunter, and I wondered if anything of significance had happened last night when the band dropped her off at her place. Making a mental note to ask for those kinds of details later, I played the hostess, offering to fill plates with food.

Taking my father's seat at the head of the table, I tore a biscuit in half and used it to scoop a large portion of the egg casserole onto my fork. Ignoring any etiquette of being a genteel Southern lady, I stuffed my face, trying to make up for not doing the same the night before and to fuel my brain to help figure everything out.

"I've been trying to come up with a clear timeline of last night," I started, finishing a bite of biscuit, "but I only have my own experience to go by. I stopped dancing, went up to the house to use the restroom, and on my way back, I overheard Azalea's distress, and found her and Harrison. But that doesn't really help figure out what happened, does it?"

Crystal raised her hand. "I'm not going to be much help since I wasn't there."

"What time was it when you left?" I asked.

She wrinkled her nose. "I wasn't wearing a watch, and I definitely wasn't paying attention to much other than my bear of a husband wanting to get a little frisky with me."

I held up my hand to stop her from adding any details. "That's enough."

Dani pulled a honeybun off the plate in front of her and passed it down. "I stayed up late last night trying to remember when I last saw Azalea or if I remembered her or Harrison disappearing from the dance floor."

"And?" I pushed.

My cousin shrugged. "I really wasn't paying attention. Blame it on these guys." She gestured around the table.

Hunter stopped mid-bite with his fork in the air. "Why is it our fault?"

"Because y'all were amazing," Cate gushed, batting her eyes at the lead singer.

"Yes, I think we've established that the members of Tailgate Down are mighty country gods," I acquiesced. "But I can't believe none of you didn't notice anything at all. Didn't any of you pay attention to the bride and groom or see either one of them take off while you were on stage?"

EJ stopped stuffing his face. "Hey, we played long after we had to. And we were playing requested songs, which isn't always the easiest. It takes effort to play covers."

I wiped my hand down my face. "I'm being rude. I didn't mean to imply you weren't doing your job or kicking butt while performing."

The lead guitarist stopped frowning and grinned. "I'll forgive you if you'll give me your bacon."

"There's an entire stack of some on a plate right in front of you," Hunter complained, pointing.

EJ raised an eyebrow, the corners of his mouth lifting in smugness. "I know. But if she's willing to give up what's on her plate, then I know she's sincere. Besides, someone else's bacon always tastes better."

"Fine," I agreed. Breaking the slice from my plate in half, I tossed each piece at him, watching him catch the first portion with his mouth and eating. He missed the second to much razzing from his friends.

Unfazed, he rescued the fumbled piece off the floor and ate it with a wink. "That's good enough for me."

Hunter chuckled into his cup of coffee. "If you asked us here thinking we could help you nail down a timeline, I don't think there's anything we can do to help. But we definitely appreciate the fuel before our long haul back home." He lifted his glass to salute me. "Sorry, Rue."

"That's not necessarily true." Levi's quiet voice interrupted, stunning us into silence. He squirmed in his seat with all the attention on him.

Hunter set his cup down. "What do you mean?"

"I think we actually could figure out the time if we can get some more information." The bassist pushed some egg around his plate with his fork.

I sat up straighter in my chair and leaned forward, forgetting about eating. "Go on. What information do you need?"

The bassist flashed his eyes in my direction and then back at his plate. "What song were we playing when you left to go to the restroom?"

The question surprised me, and I looked at Dani in the hopes that seeing her now could help me remember our moments together at the end of the night before everything went pear shaped. "It's hard to say. We danced a lot."

Cate perked up. "Ooh, I know. That song about a country girl shaking it. It's one of my favorites, and I begged you to stay."

The memory clicked into place. "Right. I like that song, too, but if I'd waited any longer to go, I would have remembered that song for a completely different and embarrassing reason."

Crystal almost spit out a sip of coffee with a laugh. "And you bet we would have never let you live it down. Let's see, Odie and I took off after that handsome man over there," she waved her thumb at Hunter, "crooned *Bless This Broken Road*. That's our special song." Color rose in her cheeks, and she ducked her head and smiled at the secret memory with her husband.

Levi listened with great intensity, nodding but not prompting. Mac pulled a small notebook out of his back pocket and asked for a pen. Not wanting to break the flow, I rushed out of my chair to find one, not caring that I tipped it over with a wooden crash onto the floor.

"Here you go." I handed the writing utensil to him and righted the head chair. "Do y'all know what you sang and when?"

"We usually keep a set list of the songs we know we're going to play," Hunter admitted. "And Mac here keeps pretty close tabs on our timing."

"Yeah, he's a little obsessed." EJ twirled his forefinger in a circle by the side of his head and mouthed, "He's crazy," to us. A piece of hash brown flew across the table and hit the guitarist in the forehead. Without blinking, he scarfed down the tasty projectile.

Mac wrote something down on his pad. "I'm not obsessed. I'm the only one who keeps us on track. I know how long each song should be and what to either add in or cut out to keep us on schedule. Without me, you'd never stop playing." He glanced up at EJ. "And think how sad that would be for all those girls you try to land at the end of every gig."

The two of them took digs at each other, and the volume of voices increased while Hunter played referee.

Exasperated, I stood up and motioned my hands in the universal sign for a time out. "Whoa, boys. Let's try and stay focused. Mac, does this mean you could build a timeline based on a few songs?"

The keyboardist grimaced and shrugged his shoulders. "Yes and no. I can say with confidence that the official reception ended at around eleven thirty because the contract was for us to perform until eleven o'clock."

Hunter pointed at him and agreed. "But since we know Harrison, we decided to keep going rather than hooking up a playlist through Bluetooth."

"Oh, right. You were taking requests of songs for those of us still partying," I recalled and pointed at my friends. "So, we know what song you performed when Crystal left. And then we know the country girl shaking song when I departed to go take care of things up at the house."

"There's a pretty big gap with who knows how many songs in between those," Dani admitted, her enthusiasm draining from her face.

"No, wait." I slapped my hands on the table. "I remember y'all played that song about cheating because I thought that was a weird request to make for a wedding reception."

"Right, it was." Hunter tipped his chair back on two legs as he thought about it. "We had a very quick debate whether or not we should play it. But since it's got such a catchy hook, we figured we'd honor the request since somebody took the time to write it down."

My eyes flashed to his. "Did everyone make requests by writing it down?"

Mac stopped taking notes. "We left scrap paper on the side of the stage and a pencil. They'd write down the name of the song and put it in an empty guitar case, and then I'd pull out the requests. We sometimes do that to challenge ourselves."

"But ultimately, we trust you to accept the

requests or not. You're a good musical director, dude." Levi clapped Mac on the back.

Any other time, I'd appreciate all the bro love flying about, but it wasn't helping me sort out the problem of who hurt Harrison. "Do you still have the requests?" I pressed.

Hart, the band's drummer, pushed his empty plate away from him. "Honestly, tearing down and packing up last night was a mess. By the time they let us go, we just wanted to get out of there."

"It's possible we tossed those slips of paper in somewhere, but it'll take us getting home and unpacking before I can look." Mac shot an apologetic glance my way.

Dani raised her hand, and I did my best not to shout at her in impatience to just speak. Once I called on her, she offered her own idea. "We were all there. If we put our heads together, maybe we could figure out which songs were played. That would give us something to go by and try to match the time."

"If only we'd been taking pictures of each other with our phones," I lamented.

Cate brushed off my regret. "We were having fun without them, like in the good ol' days. Plus, all our phones were in our purses at the table. If anybody did capture pics or videos, my bet is the county sheriffs will figure out how to collect them."

Mac turned to a clean page in his notebook. "Okay, let's assume we started free playing around half-past eleven. What songs can we remember?"

It took all of us making suggestions or clarifying each submission through our personal recollections of the moments. Music proved to be a powerful tool to help jog memories, and a list slowly formed.

"I can work on guesstimating the time on the ride home based on what we have, even though there are a few gaps," Mac offered after we ran out of songs.

"There's one song missing that's the most important." I faced Hunter. "What's that one that goes like this." I hummed what I could remember. "Oh, it's on the tip of my tongue. It's a song that What's-Her-Name who won an award this year sang."

"Hum it again," Mac asked.

Closing my eyes and concentrating, I repeated the same tune of the slow song. "It's about a space cowboy."

"Oh, that's Kacey's song we played," EJ interjected. "And there's technically a comma between *space* and *cowboy*. It's not about a cowboy riding around in space."

"But I don't understand," Dani commented. "Why's it important, Rue?"

The tune played again in my head, and I pictured light from the reception area filtering through the bushes and casting shadows behind the wedding party's table. I hadn't been paying attention to the lyrics, but I wouldn't be able to hear the music without thinking of that critical moment.

"Because I heard y'all playing it when I found Azalea and Harrison."

My confession caused a hesitant hush to fall over all of us. During our lively conversation trying to build the entire night's list of songs, we'd lost track of why we were doing it in the first place.

Mac broke the silence first by clearing his throat. "That will be the last one on our list since we barely started playing anything else before we noticed something was wrong." He jotted down the title.

"Have you heard anything from Gloria about how Harrison's doing? Or what happened with Azalea?" Crystal asked me.

I shook my head. "Gloria's not answering her texts. I'm holding out hope that no news is good news when it comes to Harrison. I plan to go to the hospital after I clean up."

"We'll help with that before we head out." Mac

closed his notebook and shoved it in his back pocket.

The clattering of plates and dishes replaced our chatter, and all of us brought stuff into the kitchen. With the tiny sink, we couldn't all do the cleaning, so I shooed the boys out with reassurances that the rest of us could handle things.

"Besides, I can't risk having y'all ruin our cast iron skillets by stripping their seasoning. You guys get on the road and get back to me with whatever timeline you come up with," I insisted.

After hugs and reassurances that I would keep them up to date on Harrison and Azalea, I waved goodbye at the door and ignored my desire to flop down on the nearest couch in exhaustion. A flurry of activity and conversation pulled me back into the kitchen.

"Them boys are definitely something to look at. And that one called Mac, well, he's just a heap of handsome. Someone in his family brought him up right," Granny Jo crowed, her corporeal form practically vibrating with appreciation.

"Are you really going to the hospital today?" Crystal asked, scooping leftovers into a plastic container.

I nodded. "I want to find out how Harrison is

plus to check on Azalea. Luke figures they might have taken her in for questioning last night." I checked my spell phone again. "I can't believe Gloria hasn't texted me back. I hope that doesn't mean something's gone wrong.

Dani stopped scrubbing down the pan in her hand. "Why don't you go ahead and go. We've got things covered in here."

Not wanting to trample on their goodwill but also chomping at the bit to find out more, I rocked back and forth on my feet. "Y'all sure?"

Granny floated over to me and spoke in a calming tone. "Friends in distress are more important than a few dirty dishes. You did good in there this morning. It'll be interesting to see how it all fits." She snapped her towel at my behind. "Now, git on outta here."

Grabbing the last piece of bacon left, I didn't wait for them to change their minds. Once in the car, I debated whether to go back to my cottage to fix my appearance or to head straight to the hospital.

Mind made up before I could think twice, my tires squealed on the pavement as I tore out of the driveway and headed in the direction of the hospital.

CHAPTER SIX

O nce I parked the car, I realized my mistake of coming to the hospital empty-handed. Gripping the steering wheel, I bit my lip in indecision whether or not to go down the street to the nearby drugstore to at least buy a card for Harrison. At the same time, I wanted to see Azalea and press for more information as soon as possible.

While caught in between choices, I detected Tara rushing out of the hospital sliding doors, a bouquet of flowers clutched in her hands. Her face was blotchy as if she'd been crying, and I got out of my car to intercept her.

"Tara, hey. Where are you going?" I called out.

She stopped mid-stride and stared at me with

wide eyes, resembling a deer caught in headlights. "What? Oh, Ruby Mae." Her eyes flitted away from me and her feet were aimed in the direction of her car. "I...I was just leaving." She paused, as if waiting for me to let her go. When I kept my focus on her, she plucked at one of the flowers in the bouquet. "Ms. Robin needs me back at the shop."

I shut the door of my car and approached her. "When did you hear about Harrison? I'm guessing you just came from seeing him. Is he okay?"

Tara's bottom lip trembled. "I didn't stick around very long, but I could tell things weren't great. I heard them say something about internal bleeding and loss of blood." A stray wind blew a strand of her hair in front of her face, and she brushed it back with a shaky hand.

"You didn't stay to find out?" I pointed at the bouquet. "Why didn't you leave those for him?"

She kept her eyes on the flowers, refusing to look at me. "Things were pretty hectic up there and I didn't want to get in the way. I just hope..." she trailed off. A single tear ran down her face, and she dashed it away and sniffed. "Here, if you're going to visit, will you take them up with you?"

I tried to refuse the bouquet she thrust in my face and encouraged her to go with me instead. "I'm sure his family would like to know how much you care."

She shook the flowers at me, and the cellophane crinkled with the force. "No, I'd just be in the way, and I don't think it would change anything." When I accepted the bouquet, she took two small steps and stopped. "Tell them they're from Ms. Robin and that she hopes Harrison has a speedy recovery."

I wanted to ask her why she didn't attend the reception, but she ducked in and out of the other cars parked around us and disappeared too fast. Gripping the flowers, I considered for a long second claiming them as my gift but came to my senses quick enough to stop in the souvenir shop on the bottom floor to purchase a small teddy bear holding a "Get Well" sign.

The elevator doors opened on the third floor, and I stepped out into the hallway, reading the signs to point me in the right direction. Loud voices arguing captured my attention, and I walked around the corner to find Azalea, dressed in yoga pants and a baggy shirt with her hair still in a messy form of her wedding updo, yelling at her parents.

"Don't even pretend that you care, Mother. I don't even know why you both came here in the first place." Azalea placed her hands on her hips and stared them down with a heated glare.

Her father held his hands up in front of him. "Let's try to calm down—"

"Do not tell me to calm down as if there's something wrong with me!" Azalea shrieked. She whipped a finger at her mother. "You stood there the night of the rehearsal dinner and begged me not to marry Harrison. Tried to bribe me with a promise of unlimited money to invest in my business."

Her mother covered her heart with her hand. "It was a terrible thing to do, and we're so sorry."

Azalea's eyes narrowed. "I think apologies are entirely too late when my *husband*," she spat out the word, "is lying in that room. He almost died. On our wedding night. And you, Dad." She shook her head and looked down at the floor, allowing her long hair to cover her face. Her hands clenched in and out of fists. When she looked back up, tears streamed down her cheeks. "I am disappointed in you the most. Even after Harrison offered to pay you back for all the money you put into the wedding. After he made the efforts to mend the bridges between all of us. You still stood up in front of all our family and friends and gave that horrible toast."

Regret passed like a shadow over her father's

face, and his shoulders fell a little. He opened his mouth to say something but sighed instead. After his quiet pause, he straightened to full height. "I'm not even sure where he would have gotten that money unless you provided it for him."

"Get out!" Azalea screamed, rushing to the space behind her parents and planting her hands on their backs. "Get out, and don't come back," she insisted, pushing them forward and in the direction of the elevators where I stood gawking.

Her mother squirmed. "Young lady, unhand us. You may have your reasons to be upset, but there is no excuse for making a spectacle of yourself."

I dodged out of the way and waited nearby, just in case my friend needed me. Gloria appeared out of nowhere and stood at my elbow. When Azalea spotted the two of us there, she regained her composure but maintained control of the situation.

Crossing her arms over her chest, she spoke in a cold but firm tone. "Mom, Dad. Thank you for all you've done for me. But you are no longer welcome in my life. No, let me rephrase that. In my husband's and my life. Please leave."

The elevator doors opened, but nobody else dared to enter inside. Azalea's father glared back at his daughter. "We'll go for now. But we'll talk about all this later when you've calmed down."

The newlywed bride's face turned a shade between red and purple, but she refused to rise to the bait. Keeping her lips pursed shut, she stood her ground until the doors closed. The second the motor whirred taking her parents away, our friend collapsed on the cold hospital tile in a heap of sobs.

A nurse in scrubs rushed out from behind the desk and came over with a damp washcloth and a tissue. "There now, honey. Sometimes you gotta stand up for yourself." She wiped away Azalea's tears and gave her the tissue, placing the cloth on the back of her neck. "Don't you worry about nothing else except seeing your man get better."

"Thank you so much," Gloria uttered, taking over the job of holding the washcloth.

The nurse with the name tag "Angel" pinned above her heart told us it was her privilege to help out. "There's a single bathroom right down that hallway, third door on your left. Why don't you take her in there and let her cry her eyes out or whatever she needs," she suggested.

I locked the door behind us and stood at the ready for Azalea. Gloria sat her friend down on the toilet seat and brushed a hand down her hair. "It'll be okay," she murmured.

"How?" Azalea cried, balling up the tissue the nurse had given her. "My brand-new husband is in a hospital because someone stabbed him."

Gloria blanched and swallowed hard. "Harrison's a strong man. You know he'll pull through."

Azalea pushed her friend's hand away. "No, none of us know that for sure. He's been intubated and doesn't even know I'm here for him. I just wish I knew this would all turn out okay." She burst into a new set of tears, and the two of us gathered around as close as we could despite our unhygienic settings. We waited for her whimpers to turn into sniffs before speaking.

I pulled the trash can over and perched on top of its metal cover. "You're right, we don't know anything for sure. None of us are psychics, and I am definitely not going to go searching for a crystal ball to try and predict your future."

Gloria half snorted but stopped herself, unsure of whether or not Azalea would get the joke or even want to laugh. We both let out the breaths we held when the new bride giggled.

"You sure you don't have another one stashed away somewhere on that big family property of yours?" Azalea asked. The partial smile she managed dropped again. "It's driving me crazy not having Harrison here to help me through all this."

The cellophane wrapped around the flowers crinkled in the following silence, and I tossed them into the sink. "They're from Ms. Robin, I guess. I ran into Tara in the parking lot."

"I saw her hovering about," Gloria confirmed. "But the doctor was giving Harrison's update, so I guess she didn't want to intrude."

My fingers stroked the soft felt of the teddy bear meant for him. "How is he? What's the latest news?"

Azalea placed her head in her hands. "The knife punctured his spleen bad enough that he needed surgery. My husband was in surgery and I wasn't here for any of it. It's hard to follow the doctor when she's saying so many words I don't understand, but I think he had a lot of internal bleeding. He coded on the table." Her entire body shook as the enormity of it all overwhelmed her.

My heart sank. "Oh, Azalea."

Gloria crouched down and hugged the new bride's shoulders. My friend looked up at me with eyes rimmed with red. "They're keeping him sedated right now, so he's not able to respond. It's a waiting game until they can wake him up and make sure the surgery worked."

A new round of crying echoed off the tiles in the bathroom. Gloria unrolled a large bunch of toilet paper and handed it to her distraught friend. I wiggled my fingers to receive some, snotting into the fluffy mass. After shared grief, Azalea groaned and drew in stuttering breaths, trying to pull herself together again.

"I have to say, I never thought I'd ever see the inside of a police station. Or county sheriff's office. Wherever it was they took me." She balled up the used tissue and tossed it into the toilet beneath her. "My wedding dress is now being kept as evidence. There's blood on the fabric. I didn't even notice it until they brought me to the station. I guess it was on my hands, and I wiped them on my dress, ruining it."

"You know, I think Ms. Robin would make you a new replacement if you asked her," I suggested, unsure if it was a good idea or an unkind one.

She stared at the floor. "I know everybody was thinking that I'm the one who stabbed him. At least, that's how it felt last night as they were taking me away and not letting me go with Harrison in the ambulance." Her tear-stained face lifted as she met my sympathetic gaze. "I'm all he has. His parents are gone, and he's been on his own for such a long time. I'm his family, and they think that I would do something to ruin all that."

Gloria petted Azalea's head and spoke in a soothing tone. "They were doing their job, sweetie. You were the one to find him, so they had to ask you questions."

Azalea shook her head. "But they kept asking me all these things, and I think they were trying to trip me up to see if my story would change. At least my parents did one thing right to support me by sending the family advocate to get me out of there as fast as possible."

As much as I loathed her parents, they were smart to retain a lawyer trained in magical law as well. Although they could work within the mortal system of judgment, hopefully Azalea's advocate would be prepared to help her should the entire situation cross over into the magical realm of justice.

"That's at least one positive thing," I agreed.

The bride snorted. "It doesn't erase the rest of their behavior. And I meant it. I won't be letting them come around us again." Her eyes flitted between Gloria and me, and neither of us contradicted her. Words said in emotional moments shouldn't be taken as final. But in the case of Azalea's parents, I'm not sure I would try to talk her into making peace in the long run.

We sat in silence a few more minutes, and I dared to ask the question at the forefront of my thoughts. "You don't think your parents had something to do with what happened?"

Gloria's eyes widened. "They're bad, but I don't think they're monsters like that, right Azalea?"

The new bride squirmed on the toilet seat. "I won't lie, that thought occurred to me. But as angry as I am with them, I can't imagine that they would threaten my own happiness by trying to have Harrison..." She didn't need to complete the sentence with the word *killed*. We all felt the gravity of her meaning.

I replayed Azalea's verbal sparring in the hallway. "What did you mean Harrison tried to pay your parents back?"

"Oh, that." She used the handrail screwed into the wall to pull herself off the toilet, tossing the wet, crumpled paper from her tears and flushing it away. "It was a last-minute idea he had after I told him what my parents said at Spinner's. It's also why we ran into him at the Tiki Tavern the night before our wedding when you were helping me try to forget the awful conversation."

It took me a few seconds to connect all the dots. "Harrison was getting money from the Tiki?" My voice rose in volume, and I tried to picture the fun-loving owner and my former boss giving our friend cash to pay off his soon-to-be in-laws. "Yeah, that's something Roscoe would do."

"But he's on one of his fishing trips, so he can't be reached. It's why my father thinks Harrison might have stolen it." She gripped the sides of the sink and stared at her reflection in the mirror. "They choose to see the absolute worst in him when everyone who knows him sees the best. The amount of money he took was the amount he's given Roscoe over time to buy a partnership into the business. He's even been helping to research what it would take to franchise the bar."

A genuine smile spread on my lips. "Roscoe's always dreamed of that. And Harrison would be a perfect partner to help him achieve it and run things." I scooted off the trash can and got close enough to rub her shoulder. "You chose a very good man, Azalea. And I know life might not be fair, but there's no way Harrison doesn't pull through. When he wants something, he goes after it. And he definitely will fight for you."

Gloria joined me, standing on the other side of the bride and embracing her. "That's right."

Azalea fought back another onslaught of tears. She looked in the mirror. "Look at us. We're an absolute mess."

With laughter through the tears, we cleaned ourselves up. Together, we stood guard in Harrison's room and waited for him to win his battle and wake up.

CHAPTER SEVEN

F or the next couple of days, life moved on for everyone but Azalea and Harrison. Dad sent me out to inventory an estate for the family business. Although the house of the deceased hadn't been that big, they had packed it full of belongings that took me the majority of a day to come up with a comprehensive list of the items.

Seeing Harrison laid up in the hospital added to the haunted images that flashed in my head, keeping me awake at night and a little jumpy during the day. Add to that a morning that turned into almost an unexpected full day of work, and I was heading home bone-weary. The truck trundled down the road until I passed the dress shop. Before I got too far away, I executed a U-turn and parked across the street from Ms. Robin's business.

The bells on the door jingled when I entered, and I walked into the same room we'd been so happy in not too long ago. I waited by the counter, not wanting to interrupt Ms. Robin if she was working. But if she had a moment free, I had a couple of questions for her.

"Please excuse me," the designer called out from the back of the room. "I was in my office, and...Ruby Mae. How nice to see you again."

"You, too, Ms. Robin. I was wondering, are you busy right now?" Even with no clients in the store, I didn't want to presume she wasn't working.

"Nothing that won't wait for later." She gestured for me to join her on the couch where we'd sat before to admire the wedding dress. "I've been hearing bits and pieces from different sources, but I'm hoping you can fill me in on what's true. I can't believe anyone thinks that sweet Azalea would have stabbed her new husband."

"Is that what's being spread around?" I frowned, cursing the clucking hens who were talking out of turn under my breath. "Azalea didn't do it. But I'm afraid her dress might have been a casualty."

I watched for Ms. Robin to react in distress about

the destruction of her work, but she waved a hand in front of her face. "In the long run, that's just some fabric and thread. It's nowhere near as important as someone's life being ruined. Speaking of, how's Harrison doing?"

Settling into the back of the couch, I readied myself to fill her in on the details all the way to the present, but Tara called out her boss's name. "How do you want me to list the rack of dresses on the back left-hand side of the storage room? Are they bridal wear or formal?" The assistant caught sight of me and stopped. "Oh, I'm sorry. I didn't know we weren't alone."

"It's okay, Tara. Sit down with us. Ruby Mae was getting ready to give us details since the two of us missed everything." Ms. Robin pointed at the nearby cushioned chair.

"Actually, I'm glad you're here, too, Tara." I shifted in my seat. "Before I share anything, I wanted to ask if either of you saw anybody or anything out of the ordinary when you were helping the bride get ready for the ceremony?"

Ms. Robin tapped the corner of her mouth. "Not that I can recall. However, the mother of the bride seemed rather chilly about her daughter's wedding day."

I rolled my eyes. "That's a whole different rodeo. Neither of you saw someone that wasn't supposed to be hanging around or seemed like maybe they were up to no good?"

Tara shook her head no but kept her mouth shut. The owner of the shop agreed. "No mustache-twirling villains lurking about that I took notice of. And Tara, you left right after the ceremony started, right?"

"Was something wrong? I thought Gloria told me you were going to hang around to help out with anything that might need fixing before official photos or the reception?" I pressed, a little disappointed in a friend from the coven letting down Azalea on her important day.

"I wasn't feeling that well," Tara uttered. Her hand lifted to her neck, and she worried her forefinger back and forth under her chin. "Ms. Robin said she'd take care of things."

The designer smiled with sympathy at her assistant. "I've had a lot of late nights out with my friends, too. But I guess she didn't recover as well as you did, Ruby Mae."

We'd encountered Tara at the Tiki Tavern when we finished medicating Azalea with booze the night before her wedding. Of course, we'd included her in the final shots since she was already there. But we'd managed to rally for our friend's entire event.

I cocked my head to the side, observing the mouse of a girl, and she drew in a quick breath. "How's Harrison?" she exhaled. "I heard he's still not doing well, but I hope that's just a rumor."

The tip of my nose itched, and I rubbed at it while considering how much to share with her. Gloria had kept me up to date as much as possible. I'd relieved my friend of staying with Azalea at the hospital a couple of times, but the determined bride refused to leave her husband's side for any considerable length of time.

"It's not good. I don't understand medical speak, but from what I did get, Harrison's life still isn't completely in the clear. The blade punctured his spleen." I pointed at my left side under my ribs and toward my back. "When they removed it, they had to perform surgery on him. I guess he had a significant amount of internal bleeding and he coded on the table. It's ironic considering only a little blood leaked out from the original wound. Although a little got on me in the process of trying to help Azalea."

"That's terrible," Ms. Robin exclaimed.

"Oh no," gushed Tara, covering her mouth with both hands and sprinting away.

"I think the whole blood thing makes her queasy. She doesn't like it when she pricks her own finger," Ms. Robin explained. "But that sounds utterly terrible for Harrison. Is he awake now?"

I shook my head. "He's still got tubes and stuff covering his mouth and nose. They're going to try and assess in the next couple of days how things are going. He's still at risk that they haven't stopped all the bleeding."

Ms. Robin leaned forward and rested her elbows on her knees, clasping her hands together. "That means they won't be able to ask him if he saw who did it. I'll bet that's why people are talking and saying that it was Azalea. That's the only information anybody has, and they're running with it."

Impressed with how quickly she'd come to the conclusion on her own, I risked showing a few of my cards to her. "I told the lieutenant when she interviewed me that I didn't think Azalea did it, and she said she'd be relying on facts and not rumors. So, that's definitely a good thing. I'm sure she'd like Harrison to be coherent so he can give his account, but in the meantime, I'm truly hoping she's building a list of plausible culprits."

Ms. Robin cocked an eyebrow at me. "I'm guessing you've already started a list of your own since you boldly asked me if I'd seen anybody. Knowing you, you're not one to rest on your laurels when you could be looking into things yourself."

"You're a genius in real life as well as with a needle and a thread," I complimented her. "I've been trying to be patient, but the longer time goes on without a better suspect, the more likely it is they might try to implicate Azalea."

The designer patted my knee and pushed herself off the couch. "If character reference meant anything, I would march right into their station and tell them there's no way that sweet girl would raise her pinky finger against her husband. I've never seen anybody so well-matched other than me and my Buster."

I stood as well and made my way toward the door. "I've known Harrison a long time. We've got work history together, and there was a time when I would have placed a considerable sum betting against him ever settling down. But after he met Azalea, I marveled at how much he changed for the better."

She clutched my wrist and stopped me from moving. "Then that's where you need to start."

"Pardon?"

"With Harrison's past," she explained. "If he

wasn't a man into settling down, then chances are he had a wandering eye. Perhaps there's someone in his past who wouldn't want him to get his Happy Ever After."

I doubted any of the bartender's former one-night stands would care an ounce if he got married. But maybe Ms. Robin was right. There could be a rotten apple or two in Harrison's past worth consideration.

"Thank you for the suggestion. It's actually really helpful," I said, opening her front door. "If not anything else other than to give me something useful to focus on."

Ms. Robin blushed. "If I was younger, I'd join you on your crusade. As it is, I'm making the first moves to ready the business for its final days. Have your dad or uncle contact me, and I'll make an appointment for you guys to come in and give me some assessments and estimates."

"With pleasure. Thanks again." I stepped out onto the sidewalk with a little more pep in my step than when I'd entered. I recalled a favor I was supposed to do for Azalea and turned on my heels and went back inside.

"Did you forget something?" the owner asked.

I tapped the side of my head. "I've been a little

tired lately. It completely slipped my mind that I was supposed to thank you for the pretty flowers you sent to the hospital."

Ms. Robin frowned. "Flowers? But I didn't order any to be delivered."

"Oh." I told her about running into Tara and the explanation that went with the bouquet I was made to take to Harrison's room. "I thought they were from you. At least that's what I was told."

The designer heaved a long sigh. "I'm sure she meant well, and I'm happy to pay her back for whatever she spent. Her focus has been slipping lately. I know a fake excuse when I hear one, and I know she could have stayed to help during the photos. But since I didn't mind helping Azalea, I thought why not let Tara go home and pull herself together." She looked off into the distance as if reliving some memory. "Sometimes we girls need a moment to regroup."

It was a simple enough explanation, and one I should have been satisfied with. After saying a second goodbye and hopping in my truck, I filed away the assistant's strange behavior as disappointing. Pulling back onto the street, I aimed the truck in the direction of Jewell, NC, hoping to get some good food with a side of good advice from my family on what happens next.

"I DON'T WANT YOU GETTING INVOLVED. I MEAN IT, Ruby Mae." My father slammed a box of stuff down on the wooden table in the middle of the storage barn.

"But Dad." If he wanted to act like an overbearing, unreasonable parent, then I had no problem whining like a child. "Me and my friends have a better chance at narrowing down who might have wanted to hurt Harrison since we know him and his wife better. We'll think of things the county sheriffs won't. And if you'd let me go raid our vault, I'll be there's something in there that could help us discover the truth."

My father stopped moving inventory around. "Now you're out of line and you know it," he grumbled. "We don't experiment with the magical items stored safely away from the human world in our secret family safe."

I shifted a box out of the way to clear room on the table. "That's not completely true," I mumbled.

"But you're right. I can take care of things on my own."

Dad halted and leaned against the top of the cardboard. "Butter bean, you've got to try and let things run their course sometimes. I know it couldn't have been easy for you to see Harrison's body hurt the way he was on the ground or laid up in the hospital. But you stickin' your nose where it doesn't belong is a surefire way to get sticker burrs in your snout. Just ask Bobby."

The dog, who'd been lying by the door and keeping watch to make sure Rex the Rooster wasn't nearby, perked up and looked at us. His tail thumped on the ground in a quick, happy rhythm.

Something bumped up against my leg, and I reached down to pick up Buddy the barn cat. "Hey, boy. Are you afraid of the rooster, too? If he gives you too hard a time, you just come knocking on my door and I'll take care of you."

Dad snorted. "Good luck trying to tame a wild cat into being domesticated."

Buddy lifted his mustached face and demanded pets. "Oh, yes. He's a fierce beasty who never gets regular attention from you or Uncle Jo." I set the cat down to let him chase something scampering off in the distance. "Put on your 'To Do' list to call Ms.

Robin. She says she wants to get an assessment done sooner rather than later. I think what happened to Azalea might have affected her more than she let on."

"Or she's tired and wants to enjoy the rest of her life. I understand that emotion." My father stooped and acted as if he would drop the last box at any moment. He grabbed his back and bellyached.

"Quit your grousin', old man. There's lots of life in you, and I ain't buying what you're selling." I tossed a dirty rag at him and guffawed when it hit him square in the face.

"You will so pay for that." He picked up the first box and placed it where he'd moved the last one, playing an odd game of storage Jenga. "You coming up to the big house for dinner tonight?"

"I think so," I admitted, too tired and lazy to fix my own food at home. My stomach growled loud enough, the dog lifted his head again. "Now I know so," I chuckled.

Dad peeled back the cardboard panels but stopped. "You know what? I think these can wait until tomorrow. Let's you and me head up there now. We can enjoy some sweet tea while rocking on the porch, and you can fill me in on your plans."

I raised an eyebrow. "I thought you were telling me to stay out of things."

He scoffed and clicked off the light, prompting Bobby to leave the barn with his foot. "There's what I tell you and what I know you'll do. I've given you my opinion, now you have to make your own decisions. You're a big girl, butter bean. I think you can keep yourself out of trouble." With a click of a few locks and a couple of well-casted spells, he secured the barn behind us.

The engine of a car roared close enough, and I strained to spot how close it was. A dark SUV with lettering on its side made its way in our direction. Although we'd warded the storage barns more carefully after the break-in and murder, we'd pulled some of the barriers a little closer since our latest security worked pretty well.

Deputy Sheriff Caine pulled his vehicle close and rolled down his window. "I wonder if I could have a moment of your time, Ms. Jewell."

Dad tipped his head out of respect to the man's profession more than the sheriff himself. "We're about to head up to the house if you'd like to accompany us and enjoy some sweet tea."

Bobby whimpered and stuffed his body between me and my father. I struggled not to grin and pursed my lips, but I appreciated the heads up that our alarm system was definitely armed. "Why don't you join us up there," I echoed my father's invitation, trying to preserve the man's safety.

Caine shut off the engine. "This isn't a social call. I've read through your interview with the lieutenant, and I have questions."

"Which my daughter would be happy to answer, but not here," Dad insisted.

"This is an active investigation, and she'll answer my questions wherever I choose to ask them." The sheriff unbuckled his seatbelt and threw his sunglasses on top of his dashboard.

Bobby leaned into my father, his high-pitched whine almost piercing our ears. A slight clucking alerted me to the danger heading our way. Dad and I checked our immediate radius to make sure we weren't in the pathway of destruction.

I held up my hand to encourage Caine to stop moving. "If I were you, Deputy Sheriff, I wouldn't get out of the car."

With determination, he ignored me and opened the door, stepping one foot onto the ground. With a cocky swagger, he got all the way out and walked toward us. "And I'm issuing you a warning that you can't threaten—Agh!" He yelled, gesticulating wildly as something pecked at his ankles.

"Told you," I crooned with an enormous amount of satisfaction permeating my entire being.

Rex the Rooster streaked out of nowhere in a frenzy of feathers, flapping wings, and a sharp beak. The bird attacked the unwanted visitor with single-minded focus, and Dad and I took the opportunity to move away and get a clear path up to the house. Bobby took off ahead of us, and I yelled at the traitor leaving us behind.

"What the heck is it?" the sheriff shouted.

I pointed at the bird who had the man cornered against his own vehicle. "That's Rex. He's a brahma bantam, which is why his legs are so fluffy with feathers."

Caine attempted to push the rooster off with one foot, but it left his other leg vulnerable to pecking. "I don't care about its variety. Get it off of me."

"I did warn you not to get out of your car," I reminded him. "If you'd taken my father up on his offer, you could have been sipping iced tea on our porch." Walking backwards, I waved. "As it is, you'll have to get yourself out of trouble. Come see me if you still want to talk."

Taking advantage of the attacked sheriff being the rooster's target, Dad and I skedaddled up the back yard toward the house. It took the deputy sheriff a good twenty minutes to figure out how to get back inside of his car before he drove right past our house. Dad and I rocked and watched his tail-lights disappear down our driveway.

"Guess he'll find another time to ask you questions," my father teased. "And butter bean?"

"Yeah, Dad?" I leaned back in my chair and turned to face him.

He raised his glass in the air. "After that display, I'm reminded of how well the local authorities did with your uncle. You do what you need to do if you think it'll help your friend with my blessin'."

He waited until I clinked my glass against his. Pleased as punch, we sat in companionable silence until the light faded and the cicadas sang.

CHAPTER EIGHT

Seagulls squawked and hovered a little too close while Gloria, Cate, and I snacked on a plate of fries. We sat under an umbrella on the patio of Ellie's Diner like old times, enjoying the roll of the ocean on a sunny day. A short man with a few wisps of hair decorating the top of his mostly bald head and wearing a red-and-white checkered apron opened the screen door and brought us a basket of fried pickles with a side of ranch dressing.

"We didn't order these," Gloria stated with a hungry eye on the appetizer.

The man whipped the towel off his shoulder and wiped sweat from his face. "They're on me. I haven't seen you girls in such a long time, now that you two have moved on from your jobs next door." He kissed me on the cheek first before planting one on Gloria and pointed at the larger structure of Riki's Tiki Tavern towering over the old joint Pops had run with his wife for the beach crowds for over forty years.

"We're lucky we even managed to get a table at all, now that you've been featured on that travel eating show. Our little local gem has had the spotlight turned on it, and all the tourists want to eat here." I beamed at the humble owner who wanted nothing more in life than to serve good food in a great location. "We're so proud of you, Pops. Ellie must be over the moon."

A little sadness dampened his enthusiasm. "She's frustrated because I've made her cut back on her time in the kitchen. But she shouldn't be running herself ragged trying to make everything all the time. We've trained good people over the years, and she deserves a little rest."

I'd heard through my friends who still worked in the beach restaurant and bars about Ellie's health. But I knew the tough old bird would fight tooth and nail before giving up control of her baby to anyone but her husband.

I took Pops' hand in mine. "You'll give her our love, won't you?"

A little moisture rimmed his eyes. "She'll be sorry she missed you. And if you hear anything about Harrison, you'll let me know. We've set up a small jar at the register up front for donations to help him out when he recovers and gets back home."

Standing up, I embraced the short lump of love and kissed his bald forehead. "You're too sweet, Pops."

He blushed two shades of red, but the merry twinkle returned to his eyes. "Y'all make sure you order whatever you want, and I'll send Wesley out here like you asked in a few." With quick steps, he disappeared back inside.

Cate sipped on her water. "We need to come here more often. It's been ages since we hung out on this patio."

Gloria agreed and wiped a finger down the side of her glass, making patterns in the condensation. "Remember that time when we wanted burgers at two in the morning after a full night of working at the Tiki? And Harrison thought it would be a good idea to come over here and make burgers?"

I groaned at the memory. "What were we thinking? We basically broke in and helped ourselves."

"We weren't thinking," Gloria snorted. "We were in our cups and every idea seemed brilliant."

Cate's head turned back and forth between Gloria and me. "I don't remember you telling me this before. What happened? The place is still standing, so I'm guessing you didn't burn it down."

"We did not," I admitted. "But we did get the cops called on us, and Pops and Ellie were woken up and had to come. There's nothing like the threat of being arrested to sober you up."

Gloria nodded. "We thought they'd be so mad at us."

"But they weren't. Ellie and Pops insisted they had given us permission to stop by after work." I popped a fried pickle in my mouth. "Once the cops left, Ellie gave us what for, but not for breaking into her place. She was mad because we hadn't made the burgers the way she does."

"And then she instructed us how to do them right before she and Pops made us all food before sending us home," Gloria finished with a shake of her head. "Yeah, we definitely need to come back here more often. I'd forgotten how good they were to us."

A plate of sliders appeared in front of us. "And that their food is pretty good as is the staff they hire," Wesley interrupted, pulling over a chair and plopping down on it. "Pops told me to bring these out to you and that I was on break for however long you needed me. I hope you're not here to tell me Harrison's taken a turn for the worst."

Gloria gasped and almost choked on her sip of tea. "Oh my gosh, Wes, I would have called you if something had happened."

He ruffled her hair, enjoying the annoyed smack on his arm. "I know, sis." His face sobered. "You've been a huge support for Azalea and barely left her side. I'm glad to see you out and about."

"I kidnapped her," I said, raising my hand. "She needed some fresh air. Well, she needed a shower first or the air around us wouldn't be so fresh right now." A fry hit the tip of my nose and fell conveniently into the ketchup on my plate.

"With Azalea's parents being banned, Azalea has nobody else to help her. They should be on their honeymoon." She sniffed and unfolded her paper napkin to dab her eyes.

Wesley rubbed her back. "Things are gonna get better soon enough. But if there's no update, then why do y'all need to talk to me?" Since none of us had touched the sliders, he took one for himself and bit into it.

I scooted my chair a little closer and leaned in so he could hear my lowered voice. "We wanted to ask you to give us some details about Harrison's former dating life." The other two girls gave him their full attention.

He stopped chewing. "I don't see how that's any of your business."

Gloria punched his arm. "Come off it, Wes. You're Harrison's best friend, and while we," she gestured between me and her, "aren't blind to his player past, we also don't know any specific names of girls he might have gotten a little more serious with."

"And why do you," he pointed at me and his sister, "need to know?"

Cate popped off. "Drop the bro code, dude, and think about it. They haven't arrested anyone who might have done what happened to your best friend. We're talking motive here, and who else would be a better candidate than a woman he's pissed off?"

"Uh, off the top of my head, maybe Azalea's parents. They hate him and have tried multiple times to pay Harrison to not marry their daughter," Wesley exclaimed.

I narrowed my eyes. "How many times?"

Recognizing his slip up of sharing, Gloria's brother frowned. "Enough that it took a whole lot of effort on my part not to deck her father the night of the rehearsal dinner."

I snorted. "You would have had to get in line behind me. They're pretty awful, but I think you would have been proud of Azalea and how she threw them out of the hospital."

"Yeah, Glo told me about that. Harrison will freaking love it when I tell him that story." He smiled in appreciation.

"Don't call me Glo," Gloria complained. "And stop dodging our question. Names, big brother. We need names."

Wesley pondered our request, delaying his response by eating a second slider. When he finished, he wiped his mouth. "To be honest, there are a fair number of girls he interacted with. Not many of them lasted long enough to remember their names. Other than Azalea, there are just two that stand out."

"And they are?" I pressed.

"One was Jane Bryce. They'd seen each other off and on since high school. Although I wouldn't classify what they had as a relationship as much as relying on each other for specific means of comfort from time to time with no strings attached." He avoided the gaze of all three of us females, concentrating on dipping a fried pickle in the ranch sauce. "I'm pretty sure she didn't do anything because last

Harrison told me, she had moved out of state and was married with three kids."

Cate wrote down the name on her napkin with a pen. "We can easily check on that. Who's the other girl you're thinking of?"

"You're not gonna like it, Glo." Wesley leaned in my direction away from his sister.

"Who?" Gloria balled her hand into a fist, preparing for the reveal.

"Cassidy Larkin."

My friend uttered a swear word loud enough for a customer at a nearby table to notice. She leaned back in her chair and stared up into the sky, counting down from ten.

"Why doesn't Gloria like this Cassidy person?" I asked, confused at the strong reaction.

When she got to one, Gloria exploded with vehemence. "Oh, just that Cassidy Larkin is my nemesis. My sworn enemy."

Wesley smirked. "They used to be best friends."

"Until I saw her for the snake she was," Gloria interjected. "She stole my boyfriend. Two of them, actually. It took me a while to see that whenever she acted like she cared and listened to me talk, like most teenage girls do about boys, what she was doing was taking mental notes and then pursuing the ones I either wanted to go out with or was actually dating."

Although Gloria and I had become friends in our early twenties, I knew she had always been a little insecure about dating. Hearing how a close friend betrayed her explained a lot and also shed light on why it was so huge that she was instrumental in bringing Azalea and Harrison together.

"So, she must have known you wanted to date Harrison," I exclaimed, making the connection.

Wesley cast an apologetic glance at his sister and explained, "Cassidy hooked him more than any other girl I'd seen. But she told him you guys were still friends and it would complicate things if you knew about them dating. So, he agreed to keep it a secret."

I was pretty sure actual steam rose off the top of Gloria's head. "That manipulative little—"

"How long did they go out and how serious did it get?" I cut her off.

Wesley rubbed his chin in thought. "They actually went out for almost six months, which was a record for him. He broke things off, but in true Harrison fashion, he would still see her from time to time."

Gloria scooted her chair even closer to Wesley.

"Was that on-again off-again time when he went out with me?"

"Maybe? I don't know, Glo, I wasn't paying that close attention." He pushed her seat away.

"What about when I introduced him to Azalea. Did he cheat on his *wife* with Cassidy?" His sister glared at him with furious intent.

"No. Absolutely not. He called me after he took Azalea out for the first time. I expected the same story as always, but it surprised me that he didn't even try to stay at her house after the first date." Wesley paused. "You know what he told me that night?"

"What?" I asked.

Wesley looked around the table at all three of us girls. "He said that he was pretty sure he'd found the woman he was going to marry. He didn't look at anyone else after that."

"Whoa." Cate put down her pen. "That's kind of big."

Gloria studied her brother with suspicion. "If that's true, then why didn't you say that in your wedding toast?"

Wesley picked up the basket of fried pickles and ate them. "He asked me not to. But I'm breaking the bro code so y'all will believe me and stop looking at me like you want to dump your drinks over my head. I'm not bringing you any refills if you do."

After a tense moment, I held up my cup. "Would you bring us some if we let you stay dry?"

Lost in thought, Gloria missed my joke. Wesley put down the basket and wiped off his hands on a napkin. He reached out to mess with her hair again but thought better of it, touching her shoulder and squeezing it. "It's in the past, Glo."

She drew in a deep breath and let it out in a loud sigh. "Maybe not. We're going to have to talk to Cassidy and make sure she didn't mind when Harrison moved on. The way I remember her, she never liked rejection."

Wesley stood. "I think it's a far stretch to consider she might have gone out of her way to hurt him at his wedding reception."

I tilted my head and scolded him. "You clearly don't know much about scorned women."

A cocky grin spread across his lips he'd once bragged no girl could resist. "I'd have to actually date them more than once to learn." Clearing off the empty food baskets, Wesley left us to our plans.

"It won't be hard to track down whether or not Cassidy still lives in the area," Cate offered.

"She does," Gloria confirmed. "She's still working

at her mother's floral shop. You know why I know that?" Her chair scraped on the wooden patio as she got up and retrieved her purse from the back of the chair.

"You've been secretly stalking her all these years, waiting for the day when you would get your sweet, sweet revenge?" I suggested, hoping to lighten her mood.

All I got for my efforts was a snort. "Not hardly. No, but I've seen Cassidy not too long ago," Gloria said with a sigh. "When I went with Azalea and her mother to interview their shop about doing the wedding flowers."

"N-o-o-o!" Cate dragged out. "Tell me that's not the shop that actually provided them. They were so pretty."

Gloria grunted, "Hmph," and left us slack-jawed in the sun.

We headed back inside and attempted to pay Pops at the register for the food he'd provided, but he wouldn't hear of it. Once we settled in my truck, we sat in awed silence. My fingers turned white from gripping the steering wheel.

"Welcome to my world, ladies," Gloria said with a sad smile. "I couldn't figure out why Azalea's mom would want to hire her daughter's fiancé's ex to provide the flowers except in an attempt to cause strife between her and Harrison."

If I'd had a shred of respect left for her parents, this new information torched it into oblivion. "That's so twisted."

"Well, her plan backfired," Cate said from the backseat.

"Oh, it definitely caused tension," Gloria countered. "More than once, I had to calm Azalea down during the months of preparation. And if I'd had any cajones, I would have marched into the shop myself and demanded that Cassidy not be involved in any of the deliveries."

I smacked the steering wheel hard enough my palm stung. "She didn't show up on the wedding day, did she?"

Gloria's jaw tightened. "I was hoping she'd know better, but that girl likes to mess with people. I kind of felt bad because I think if it hadn't been an added bonus she could bug me as well, she might not have tried so hard to get to Azalea. Out of all people, she was the one who delivered the bridal party bouquets to the suite prior to the ceremony."

What had been such a beautiful day had turned out to have so many ugly shadows. My love and admiration for Azalea increased at her ability to take everything thrown at her and still make the best of things. With a little digging, we found someone who might have done more than deliver flowers to get at her in the long run.

"Right. Let's go." I turned the key and revved the engine of Deacon's borrowed F-150. It rumbled underneath us, and as we left the parking lot, I punched the gas a little too hard, throwing gravel out from under the tires when we pulled out on the road.

Cate leaned forward and grabbed the back of my headrest. "Exactly where are we going in such a hurry?"

A sly grin crept onto my lips. I glanced in the rearview mirror at my friend. "To nip things in the bud right now."

CHAPTER NINE

T he three of us sat in the truck outside of the strip mall in front of Beach Blooms, readying for battle.

"If she's truly horrible like you said, I could always wilt all the flowers in there with a little of my magic," I offered, conjuring a tiny flame in the palm of my hand.

"No, you can't do that," Cate protested, smacking my shoulder from the backseat. "Don't take anything out on those innocent plants."

"Sometimes I think you're a little too nice, Caty-did," I teased. "You have to admit, even Nature can sometimes be cruel when she needs to be."

Gloria flipped down the visor and applied a new layer of lipstick, checking her appearance in the small mirror. "If I have to face Cassidy, I want to look good doing it." She slammed the visor back into place. "Ready, girls?"

"Ready," Cate and I replied.

An electronic bell dinged as soon as we opened the door to the shop. Beautiful flower arrangements peppered the area. If we weren't here to fight, I might be so impressed that I could buy one or two things to take back with me.

"I'll be right with you," a female voice called from the back room. "Feel free to take a look around."

Gloria cringed. "That's her. I guess her mom's not here today."

"There, that's finished." A young woman about the same age as us with blonde hair pulled back in a messy bun wiped her hands on her pink-striped apron. "The hazards of working with glitter are that it gets absolutely everywhere." She glanced up at us with a smile and stopped in her tracks. "Gloria."

"Cassidy," my friend replied in a tense tone.

The smile faded from the woman's lips for a second, but she recovered and plastered one on, speaking in an empty, pleasant voice. "How may I help you ladies today?"

"Cut the crap, Cass," Gloria demanded. "I want to know why you took the job of providing the flowers for Azalea and Harrison's wedding. Surely you had to know it would cause trouble. Or is that why you did it?"

Okay, we were going to jump straight into the deep end. I stepped to my friend's side and stood as tall as I could, raising my chin in indignation.

Cassidy blinked a couple of times in shock. "I wasn't trying to cause trouble. I was hired to do a job, and I think our shop more than fulfilled the bride and groom's requests." Her hands curled in and out of fists. "I heard what happened. I hope you can pass on our good wishes to Harrison for a fast recovery. If you want to pick something out to take to him, I'd be happy to give it to you for free."

It was hard to maintain a level of anger at her when all I observed was someone who was kind and thoughtful. But I trusted Gloria, and if she said we couldn't rely on Cassidy to be a good person, then the lady didn't deserve thoughtful consideration.

"Right. Would you like me to sign the card in your name? That way, Azalea will know they came from you." Gloria took a step closer to her former friend. "You were always good at hiding your evil deeds behind good intentions."

Instead of smirking or egging Gloria on, Cassidy

fiddled with the ends of her apron. "I think it might be best if you leave."

I cleared my throat. "It's hard to be confronted with the truth, isn't it?"

"But she's got it all wrong." Cassidy stood her ground for a moment and turned away, walking behind the front display case to get a little space between us.

Gloria closed the distance and pounded her hands on the countertop. "Oh, I was wrong about you for years. But I'm pretty sure I have you pegged."

Cassidy's shoulders slumped, and she busied herself with tidying up the rows of ribbons. "If you're so sure about me, then why even come here?"

"You were at the Wallace House the day of the wedding, right?" I asked, ready to get some answers.

"Of course. We had to deliver the bouquets to the bridal suite and the boutonnières to the men as well as set up the arrangements for the ceremony and complete the design for the reception." She stood her ground with her arms crossed. "It's what we were hired to do."

Her reply didn't sound unreasonable, but it still meant she had open access to all areas of the wedding. It wouldn't be an impossible leap to consider her sticking around during the entire event. Maybe in a fit of jealousy, she attacked Harrison.

Gloria leaned against the case. "But why you, Cass? I mean, you had to flaunt yourself in front of Azalea by delivering her bouquet right to her."

The florist's eyes got as big as the peonies in the refrigerators behind her. "That's what you think? That I took the job to torture Harrison and his bride?"

I steadied myself for a knockdown drag out fight to break out, but Cassidy hurried out from behind the counter and clasped her hands over Gloria's shoulders. "Oh, Glo, I never meant for things to go as bad as they clearly have between us. I'm so sorry."

Cate and I gawped at the interaction, shocked bystanders to Gloria's fizzling anger. Her mouth opened once or twice, but she didn't manage to say anything. For everything we'd prepared for when we came in here to confront Cassidy, none of us had expected to hear any apologies.

"You're just saying that to get out of trouble," Gloria accused. She cast her eyes to the floor. "I still don't see why you took the job in the first place."

The florist let go of her former friend with a disappointed exhale. "Because I thought that maybe I could make up for the past. That us doing a good job would be a great way to let Harrison know I wished him well. And to do something nice for your friend."

Gloria sniffed, caught between warring emotions. "That doesn't sound like the person I once knew."

"We haven't been friends for a long time. And that's my fault entirely. I destroyed something good in my life because I never believed I deserved anything good." Cassidy's voice trembled, and she reached up to her neck, pulling out a silver chain. "I still wear this every day as a reminder to be better than I was."

The rest of Gloria's anger evaporated at the sight of something meaningful to her. "That's the necklace I gave you after graduation."

"Yep." Cassidy pulled the pendant out for us to see. "It's a bird because Glo heard me say all the time how I'd like to fly away. Yet I ended up not getting very far." She stopped talking to Cate and me and turned her full attention back to her former friend. "Gloria, I really do apologize for the way I mistreated you. Losing your friendship was the worst thing that's happened to me, and I've regretted it for a long time. I hope someday, you can forgive me."

The alert from the front door chimed, and a little

girl in a frilly dress ran inside and launched herself at Cassidy's leg. "Mommy!" she cried with a great big grin.

"Hey there, munchkin. Did you have a good time with Grammy today?" Cassidy bent down and picked up the girl who got shy when she spotted all of us watching her. "And this here is the best thing that's happened to me. Gloria Jean, say hello to these nice ladies."

After a small wave, the little girl buried her head in her mother's shoulder. An older lady stepped up to peel her granddaughter off. "Come here, love bug. We'll take you in the back and get you a juice box." Before she left, she placed a hand on Gloria's arm. "I'm glad to see you two talking again." The grandmother and granddaughter disappeared into the back.

Gloria gaped after them. "Cass, you're a mom."

"I am. I mean it when I said she's the best thing to happen to me." She clutched the space over her heart. "If anyone had treated her the way I behaved towards you, I'm pretty sure I'd go to jail for hurting them."

Her exaggeration reminded me of our original purpose. It felt a little awkward bringing up the wedding day, but I needed to hear her answers.

"So, after you finished putting together all the flowers for the event, did you stick around for the reception?" I pushed, ignoring the little twinge of guilt for even asking.

Cassidy stopped smiling at her former friend. "Actually, my babysitter called me because my daughter had a stomachache. So, I left before our crew was even finished."

"And your daughter's name?" Gloria asked.

The grin returned to the florist's face. "I named her after you in the hopes that she would be as kind as you had been and to strive to be better. Jean is after my mom, the other woman I want her to grow up to be like."

Cate reached in her purse and pulled out a tissue to wipe away her tears. I didn't come as prepared, so I bit my lip in order not to lose control.

Gloria hesitated for another moment before sticking out her hand. "I accept your apology."

Cassidy blew out a huge sigh of relief. "You don't know how you've just made my entire year, not just my day. I've been waiting to say these things to you all along, but I didn't want to ruin your friend's wedding preparations by putting myself first."

"I guess I was only seeing things from my point of view," Gloria admitted.

"I get it. But whatever brought you in here today, I'm so happy we got to talk." Her body tensed as if she wanted to give her old friend a hug, but she placed her arms behind her back instead. "I hope Harrison gets better soon. Are you sure you don't want to pick something out to take to him at the hospital?"

Gloria looked around the shop as if seeing it for the first time. "You have a lot of beautiful things here. If you've got a moment, maybe you can give us some options."

When we left, the other half of the back seat was full of plants and flowers we'd purchased to take home with us or to drop off at the hospital. Cate cradled a potted peperomia with deep green ornamental leaves, already talking to it. Gloria settled the peace lily she'd picked out for Harrison between her legs in the front seat. Somewhere between the spider plant and the devil's ivy I'd gotten for Luke's house was my clivia with its bright orange blossoms with yellow middles. I pictured it sitting on the windowsill of my kitchen like my own floral fire. If I could keep it alive long enough, I might consider getting something else later on.

"That was completely unexpected and overwhelming," Gloria stated. "And I'm not sure how helpful it was."

"But you got to mend fences with an old friend. I'd say this was an incredibly beneficial," I countered, driving in the direction of the hospital to drop her off first.

We rode the rest of the trip with the radio on, half listening to the songs and half caught up in our own thoughts. I pulled the truck up to the entrance and Gloria untangled her feet without hurting the plant before picking it up.

She shut the truck door and spoke through the rolled down window. "Well, it looks like you're back to square one, trying to come up with whoever hurt Harrison."

"It was a good theory while it lasted. And I'm sure we can come up with other ideas when we get together again." I didn't want to stress her out with my growing doubt and worry for Azalea. "We've got the coven meeting coming up. Maybe all of us can go out afterwards and brainstorm."

She shot me a thumbs up. "I'll text you any updates once I get up there. Thanks for having my back."

We waited until she made it inside before driving away. Cate stayed in the backseat happy as a clam with all the plants back there, and I drove us both toward Cedar Point.

After the umpteenth advertisement on the radio, a catchy country song played, and I hummed along, singing the words when I remembered them. It dawned on me I hadn't heard back from Mac about the playlist. With no other ideas of how to find the person who hurt our friend, I took a little comfort in having at least one thing I could check on. Once I got home, I could message the band and see what they'd put together for a timeline.

Turning up the volume, I belted out the chorus and sang away my blues.

CHAPTER TEN

The timeline Mac sent me through email didn't do much other than narrow down the window of when Harrison was stabbed. It gave me a little too much smug pleasure to know the lieutenant had not reached out to the band to ask them the same thing, which meant only I had come up with the brilliant idea. But it didn't do anyone any favors to keep the useful information to myself if it didn't help find who stabbed Harrison or keep Azalea from being the number one suspect. Still, I wanted to talk with my friends after the coven meeting and see what we could come up with before handing the information over.

On the afternoon before the meeting, I begged off helping to unload another haul from a short picking trip and headed back to my place. Exhausted from a lack of consistent sleep and my brain working overtime to piece everything together, I stared up at the ceiling while lying on my bed. Sleeplessness was all too familiar. I'd gotten so used to stressing out that I couldn't rest and not resting because of the stress. I tossed and turned on top of the quilt, determined to at least do nothing if I couldn't succeed at napping.

A warm blanket was wrapped around my body when I woke up some time later. Disoriented, I rubbed my eyes and checked the time. I'd managed to fall asleep for a couple of hours. Yawning, I stretched my arms and debated dozing through dinnertime, figuring I could snack at the meeting. I almost snuggled back under the blanket when I caught the scent of something yummy.

My stomach growled, and I padded out of my room and down the hall to the kitchen, following the smell of garlic and onion. Luke stood at the stove, stirring the contents inside a pot and pouring white wine into the rest of the ingredients with a steamy hiss.

I wrapped my arms around his middle and rested my head against his back. "I thought vampires didn't like garlic."

His rumbling chuckle vibrated into my cheek. "This vampire thinks it's absolutely an essential part of good cooking and especially the risotto I'm making for you. If you're not too tired, could you cut those zucchinis into thin slices for me?" He pointed with the wooden spoon at the three green veggies lying on a nearby wooden cutting board. With a ladle, he spooned some of the hot liquid from a second pot into the first, still stirring.

I cut the zucchini like he asked, wondering what I'd done to deserve a boyfriend who cooked amazing Italian meals whenever he wanted to woo me. We hadn't had much time to see each other after the wedding with a bunch of jobs coming in for the family business and my efforts to investigate Harrison's stabbing during my off moments.

Luke had been working on a special job fixing up a vintage car for a client, which usually consumed his attention. If we hadn't had such a good night dancing together and he hadn't given his admission about his awareness of the distance between us, I might have continued worrying about us. If a tasty dinner was his way to butter me up, I had no complaints.

Never taking the wooden spoon out of the pot of risotto, my handsome boyfriend flashed me a sexy smile. "Did you get a little rest? You were pretty much out of it when I arrived. You didn't even hear me when I was calling out your name."

"Thanks for throwing the blanket over me." I snuck a slice of zucchini and ate it. "I haven't been sleeping well. I guess my body finally conked out."

He ladled some more liquid into the pot. "I'm sorry I've been working so hard. I should have checked in person rather than trusting when you told me you were okay over the phone."

"But I was okay. And you have a special job you're working on right now. I know that means you're at the garage more than usual. If I really needed you, I would have said so." Dropping the third zucchini slice when he scolded me, I closed the distance between us and hooked my arms around his middle. "Don't I look okay to you?"

Luke gave me a critical once over with intentional drama. "Hmm. You've got a little dried drool at the left corner of your mouth. Other than that, you're practically perfect," he teased, kissing the tip of my nose. "Now, bring me the rest of the zucchini you didn't eat and dump it all in. Then you can grate some parmesan cheese into that bowl on the counter."

Following his orders, I saluted him once before I

got the cheese and grater. After I finished and put the bowl beside him to add to the pot when he was ready, I opened up the cupboard to pull out dishes to place on the table.

"It's already set," Luke said with a warm smile. "If you want to go sit down and have a glass of wine, I'll bring dinner with me in a moment."

Since Dani was driving to the coven meeting tonight, I saw no reason not to indulge in a glass of chilled crisp Pinot Grigio. My boyfriend had chosen my good plates without any chips in them and had found some orange and red placemats to match my new clivia he'd set in the middle of the table. A simple salad of arugula dressed in olive oil with thin slices of parmesan on top waited to accompany the delicious meal. Pulling a bite of bread off the crusty loaf warmed and waiting in a basket underneath a towel, I sipped on wine and enjoyed the goodness of a simple moment together.

Luke carried the pot he'd been stirring over to the table and poured out the creamy Italian rice dish onto my plate. "There's plenty more, so eat as much as you want."

My mouth watered at the sight of the risotto. "I'm glad you don't mind my curves," I gushed, barely holding back from digging in until he'd served himself.

He placed the hot pot on a trivet and poured himself a glass of white wine. Lifting it in the air, he toasted, "I could quote some old Italian saying or come up with something really romantic. But all I want to say in this moment is that I love you, Ruby Mae Jewell. And each day I get to be with you is a gift. I will do better not to take that for granted."

The heat rose in my cheeks, and I clinked my glass against his. "I think that was very romantic." Although I adored when he spoke Italian to me, the truth in his words knocked me silly.

I scooped up the first bite of risotto and put it in my mouth. An obscene groan emanated from deep within, and I closed my eyes to enjoy the intense flavors. "So good."

He chuckled. "I'm glad you like it, *cara*. But if you don't mind, I'd prefer if you kept your eyes open. I've got some things to say while we eat."

If he wanted me to do a handstand or backflips, I probably would attempt either as long as I could be fed this dish the entire time. With effort, I peeled my eyes open and did my best to focus on him rather than the fantastic food.

He pushed some of the risotto around on his plate but didn't eat any. "I know I allowed it when you drank a drop of my blood not that long ago. And I don't want you to feel badly that you did. But I chose not to give you my thoughts about it then and only realized the full dangers after you did it. I confess, I should have given voice to my worries rather than brooding and regretting our actions that night."

I stopped shoveling food in my mouth. "You regret sharing your blood with me?"

He grimaced. "I know it helped you to overcome whatever force was attached to the crystal ball. And I'm glad you destroyed it in the long run, so if my blood was instrumental in that act, then I guess it's hard for me to resent it completely. But you know that there were consequences afterwards."

I put my fork down and wiped my mouth with the napkin. Sliding my chair back, I made my way to the other side of the table and waited for him to scoot back just enough for me to snuggle into his lap. No matter what we talked about tonight, I refused to have any unwelcome space between us. "Yes, I told you about all the extra sensations openly. And every time I did, you got angry."

"Not angry, Rue. Worried. There are bigger consequences than just enhanced senses for you.

And a part of me was concerned it might affect you on a cellular level." He brushed his fingertip down my cheek. "That even that small amount you ingested might have turned you."

"Into a vampire? I thought it required you draining me of all my blood and then making me consume all of it back from you. And then you'd bury me in the ground, and I would have to claw my way into my new undead life." I hoped my joke would lighten the weight of this discussion.

"Movies have not been kind to us, although blood is definitely the doorway."

Despite the need for us to talk, my stomach groaned, interrupting him. Without asking, he used his own fork to feed me some more so I could stay put. I liked being an independent girl, but it also pleased me to be pampered by my man.

"Rue, there are reasons I have not revealed to you everything about my past," he continued. "At first, I was glad that you didn't probe into it, even though I know you like to solve mysteries."

I pointed at my chest. "Who? Me?" My response earned me a playful pinch on my behind. I squirmed in his lap until he held me still and fed me another bite.

"It's for your safety that I have not told you

everything about myself. There are some secrets about my life that if delved into would set events in motion that I wouldn't be able to stop." He stopped feeding me as he got caught up in his past.

Smoothing the wrinkle between his eyebrows with my fingertip, I leaned in and placed a chaste kiss on his lips. "I know you'll do everything you can to keep me safe. But, as old as you are, you have to know that secrets can be dangerous, too."

Luke hugged me to him, and the deep breath he drew in and let out tickled my ear. "I know. It's the choice I'm making until I think that your knowing everything is the safer path. Can you at least give me that?"

It went against my very nature not to know everything. I think I'd allowed him to keep his past from me because I assumed as a vampire, there might be violent acts or other things he'd done that might scare me away. Having him insist he was keeping things from me for my safety piqued my curious nature, but I didn't want to ruin the night.

"I'll concede that you believe keeping your secrets from me is for my own good." I lifted his chin with my finger so he had to see my sincerity. "For now. But you know me well enough to know that won't last very long. You're going to need to figure out what you can and cannot tell me in the very near future. Starting with what any of this has to do with you worrying I took a drop of your blood. Not a whole body's worth. A drop."

Luke patted my behind and let me go. I took the hint and moved off his lap, taking my place across from him again. Unlike me who popped up and said things before my brain got a chance to think about my words, he liked to take his time and deliberate. I drank some more wine and ate a little of the peppery arugula salad, waiting.

"I already told you I was afraid that it could have changed you on a cellular level. That means changing your biology. It terrified me how long you remained with heightened senses. The effects of my blood should have worn off quickly, but for you, it lasted far longer." He ran a finger around the rim of his wine glass. "It proved the strength of my own blood."

"Or it demonstrated that my powerful lineage of witch blood running through me bonded with yours, and the combined magic lasted longer than you expected." I finished the rest of the cold wine in a couple of swallows. "You may be overthinking things."

His eyebrows raised. "You know, it never

occurred to me that your own blood might have been a factor. That's something I can research…" Luke trailed off, lost in a train of thought he didn't want to share.

I cleared my throat to regain his attention. "Does this mean you might stop worrying about me and keeping me at arm's length?"

Luke glared at me from across the table. Without saying a word, he got up and stalked over to my side. With his hand on the back of my chair, he waited for me to slide out of it. Finally, he wrapped his arms around me and rocked me back and forth, reminding me of the few good moments from the wedding reception.

"What are you doing?" I murmured into his chest.

He kissed the top of my head. "Closing the distance," he answered in a quiet voice, still leading me in a silent slow dance.

"Good answer," I whispered back.

Luke hadn't given me responses to all of the questions I'd been asking myself. And he created new ones for me to consider. But he gave me what I wanted most, and that would satisfy me.

For now.

CHAPTER ELEVEN

G loria stood with me and my girlfriends in place on the outer circle for the final ritual of the night. I didn't know how other covens ran things, but I kind of liked the meditation and attempt at focusing all of our energy together to put light and love out into the world. I squeezed my eyes extra tight and added a little more intent for it to affect Azalea and Harrison's lives a little sooner rather than later.

At the center of the ritual, Ebonee held up her hands. "We honor the elements, Earth, Air, Fire, and Water, and ask for balance in our lives as you live in all of us."

A little of my own magic zinged to life at the mention of my particular element. Although most witches had a mix of the elements in them, thanks to the witchy genes from my mother, I leaned so heavily to fire that I often wondered if it meant I was off balance all together. Then again, Cate practiced earth magics while Crystal's gifts with water influenced her entire life. We all lived with the powers life dealt us as best we could, and maybe relied on each other to bring stability rather than solely on ourselves alone.

As a coven, we faced each of the cardinal directions in the final salutation to close the ritual circles. Holding onto Gloria on my right side and Dani on my left, I readied myself for the little burst of power the collective passed on to each other at the very end. Tonight, I looked forward to the boost of energy to fuel us for our planned brainstorm.

"So may it be," finished Ebonee, waiting for the rest of us to repeat the phrase.

The zing of energy flowed through Dani and into me. It passed into Gloria, and she yanked her hand away with a yelp. She doubled over as if someone had punched her in her gut.

"Are you okay?" I asked, breaking the calm after the ritual had finished.

She pulled in a sharp breath and cradled her stomach. "Yeah, I think so. I knew I shouldn't have eaten that chicken salad before coming. I've been so busy staying with Azalea at the hospital, I think it might have been too old."

I held her about her shoulders. "Let one of us take you home."

"I can drive as long as I don't stop anywhere else," she reassured us. "Don't worry about me. Stick to your plan."

The coven members who stayed to check on her moved away, and I spotted Azalea's parents walking in our direction. "Uh oh. Maybe you should go right now."

"Gloria," Azalea's father called out. "We'd like to ask you about our daughter."

"Not now, sir," I insisted. "She's a little under the weather and should go straight home."

Azalea's mother stepped forward, ignoring me. "We'd like for you to convince our daughter to let us see her. We have things we need to talk through with her."

Gloria's face crumpled in pain. "After everything you put her through, I don't blame her for keeping you away. Her husband has yet to be discharged from the hospital. I think for now, you need to accept that no news is good news until she decides if she wants to connect with you again."

"Why is it that ever since that boy came into her life, she has always chosen him over us?" Azalea's father accused more than asked.

Tired of him not even listening to the most important bits, I got in his face. "Maybe because you can't see past your own discriminations. You definitely don't listen, and from everything I've seen, you don't consider or respect your daughter's own choices." I held up my hand in front of his face to keep him from saying something vile to me. "And you think you can buy her love with money. Which, if you even knew your daughter in the slightest, was never going to work."

Azalea's mother's puckered face soured even more. "I don't think any of this is your concern."

Dani, who hated confrontation and rarely stepped willingly into the fray, spoke up. "It is when you choose to be as free and open with your vitriol as you are. Now, I suggest you leave Gloria alone and think about allowing a little love and light into your own lives. Maybe then you'll appreciate what you've already lost." She put her hands together and bowed. "So may it be."

Any other time, I would high-five her for her uncharacteristic snark. But Gloria bent over and grabbed her knees with her hands as if she were going to need a bathroom. Crystal placed her body between our friend and Azalea's parents, rubbing Gloria's back. "I'm going to take you home right now."

Ebonee insisted that the lingering coven members depart and stop watching the spectacle. "Mr. and Mrs. Cunningham, I think it's best for you to allow the young lady to depart. She is clearly unwell."

Not even listening to their leader, Azalea's father fired one final shot. "If you'd be willing to help us and get our daughter to at least talk to us, we can make sure you are well compensated."

"Stan," Ebonee took him by his elbow. "You will not try to bribe one of our members. You've been asked to stop harassing her and requested to allow her to leave."

The man yanked his arm out of the leader's grip. "You risk losing our support for your position," he threatened. "Don't forget, it took you having all the right friends for you to get where you are."

The rude comment cracked some of Ebonee's cold, professional veneer, and she sneered. "But you're forgetting that I am where I am, here and now. And if you continue to dishonor the intent of our coven with your attitude and words, then I can make sure that as of right *now*, you are no longer welcome *here*."

His wife grabbed him by the sleeve of his shirt. "Come on, Stanley. Let's go."

Ebonee instructed two nearby members to make sure they didn't bother Gloria or Crystal in the parking lot. Seeing her take such quick action impressed me, and I considered my own prejudgments of her. Until I remembered how much she clamored for the crystal ball at my family home and reminded myself to be watchful and wary.

"Why is it that whenever there seems to be drama, you are present, Ms. Jewell?" she asked.

Aw, somebody replaced the stick up her behind again. "Total coincidence. And you can't blame me for their actions." I pointed in the direction Azalea's parents had departed the room in a huff.

"No, I suppose I cannot. But if I can take you away from your friends for a moment, there is something I'd like to discuss with you. With a little more privacy." She walked away, not even checking to see if I agreed to her request.

Dani waved at me. "I'll wait for you in the car. Text me if you think it's going to take more than a few minutes and I'll let the others know we'll be late." Wesley had gotten Pops to let us use his diner to meet in, and it would take a good twenty minutes to drive out to the beach from where we were.

I rushed to follow Ebonee into the office at the back of the building. In my head, I'd pictured her sitting on a huge gold throne, plotting ways to rule over all of us. Instead, I entered a room with simple office furniture with the usual filing cabinets, folders, and other mundane items.

"Sit down." She gestured at the cushioned chair in front of her desk. "Would you like something to drink? Maybe some water?" Without waiting for my answer, she drew a cold bottle out of a small fridge behind her and handed it to me.

Being in her presence activated my nerves, and I unscrewed the top and took a sip. "It's like being called into the principal's office. Can't lie, I feel like I'm gonna get detention or something." I fidgeted in my seat, trying to find any personal items to give me even a hint about the leader's personal life.

Ebonee folded her hands in front of her on the desk. "Why doesn't that surprise me? Now, I'd like to discuss what you have found out so far."

I scrambled to think of what she might be referring to and came up blank. "About what?"

"Don't play coy with me, Ms. Jewell." She leaned forward, holding me in her intense scrutiny. "You didn't allow the authorities to do all the investigating when your uncle was suspected of murder. I'm assuming you have been scheming ways to discover who we might be looking for with Harrison's unfortunate incident."

Well, grits and ghosts. I hadn't counted on her suspecting my involvement. At least not quite so early in the process. "Who says I'm doing anything?" I tipped the bottle back again, hoping I could deflect any specific questions.

Ebonee pointed at my drink. "If you give it enough time, perhaps the potion of truth I placed in that will kick in."

I spit out my mouthful and set the bottle down on the edge of her desk, staring at it in disgust. "You would give a potion to one of your coven members and not tell them? Isn't that breaking a lot of rules you love to live by?" Sticking out my tongue as far as I could, I wiped it down with the back of my hand.

"Relax, it was just a crude joke to try and break the ice with you." The leader cracked a rare genuine smile. "What, you think you're the only one well-versed in sarcasm and sass?"

My jaw dropped, and I blinked at her, unable to come up with a pithy retort. Or any response.

"Now that I have your attention, how about I

show you my hand so you know I'm sincere?" She leaned back in her chair and nodded once as if having to accept her own idea. "I've been working with Lieutenant Alwin to try and keep Azalea from being considered a suspect due to probable cause. So far, I know that only her prints were found on the hilt of the knife they collected after Mr. Dobbs' surgery."

The spell phone in my purse vibrated once with a text. Ignoring it, I responded, "She probably obscured prints from the assailant when she tried to remove it from her husband's body."

Ebonee accepted my addition to her information with a slight grunt of agreement. "Olivia had her team interview all of the vendors who had access to the space, creating a timeline of their comings and goings."

That would have been useful information before we'd confronted Cassidy. However, I didn't regret the opportunity we took to talk to her since it resulted in the first stitches to mend a friendship. My phone vibrated again, and I fidgeted under the coven leader's glare of disapproval.

"I think you and I would agree that without a clear alternative of a suspect, Azalea will be vulnerable." Something akin to regret passed like a shadow over her face. "I'd like to avoid that if possible, and I need as much information as I can get to aid her and prevent it from happening." She bounced her foot under the desk, the heel of her stiletto tapping the floor.

Seeing even a small chink in her armor eased my hesitation. "I think I understand. You and I have a similar goal, and maybe if we pool our resources, we could do more good than harm as a team?"

Ebonee scowled at my choice of words. "We are not equals, Ms. Jewell. And this would be a temporary arrangement of the flow of information. If you have something to contribute, bring it to me."

I raised an eyebrow. "And if I wanted to know something, would you tell me if I asked? Or am I going to be held accountable after the fact and get in trouble for sticking my nose where it doesn't belong, so to speak?"

"The lieutenant has been warned about your propensity to meddle. However, she has persuaded me that your close relationship with those involved could be beneficial. Olivia has been doing her best to keep you free to do what you need to do," Ebonee said.

"Hasn't stopped one of the deputy sheriffs from

showing up on our property." I smirked in amusement at Caine's defeat by our rooster.

"I didn't say she could control everything. Being that you were involved in the incident, you'll have to expect some attention. But I trust in your abilities to handle yourself." Ebonee glanced at the clock on the wall and back at my purse with my phone vibrating two times in a row. "Due to the sense of urgency coming from inside your bag, may we come to an accord so that we can both leave?"

Without the ability to check with my friends to think if it was a good idea, I took a chance. My curiosity to find out more from the official side of the investigations outweighed my desire to rebel against the coven leader. I stuck out my hand. "Deal, as long as the information flows both ways."

Ebonee's cold fingers wrapped around mine as we shook on it. "Tomorrow, I'd like for you to come back and share everything you know so far and any plans you have for any further inquiries. For now, go meet your friends at Pops' place. Eat an Ellie burger and some fries for me. It's been a while since I've been there."

For the second time tonight, I gaped at her. "How did you know?"

Her lips snaked into a grin like the Cheshire Cat's

from *Alice in Wonderland*. "I'm the coven leader. It's my job to know everything." She gestured at the door, dismissing me. "May your habit of getting into trouble keep a friend out of it. Now, please answer whoever it is that insists on messaging you on your way out."

She didn't have to ask me twice, and I shot out of the room as fast as my legs could speed walk. I almost got out of the building when I read through the barrage of texts from Dani and Gloria. Turning around, I hustled back to the office and caught Ebonee as she was locking the door.

Keeping my end of the bargain, I shared the news with her. "Harrison had internal bleeding they couldn't detect until now. The doctors took him in for emergency surgery, but it's not looking good."

"I'll alert Olivia, but you should go with your friends to the hospital." When I couldn't move out of the sheer panic gripping my heart, Ebonee approached me and placed her hands on my arms with a gentle grasp. "Go. Your friends need you."

I bolted out of the building to find Dani, hoping we wouldn't be too late.

CHAPTER TWELVE

"You gave us a huge scare, buddy." I dumped a potted plant, a box of chocolates, a large bouquet of flowers, and an even bigger teddy bear than I'd purchased at the hospital gift shop into Harrison's lap.

My friend struggled under all the items while he lay in the recliner in his living room, recovering from his emergency splenectomy only a week earlier. "They took out my spleen, Ruby Mae. I don't think that merits you stopping at every store between your home and here to get me anything."

Azalea removed all of the items except the teddy bear. "I'll have to see if we have anymore vases left. It's beginning to look like a greenhouse in here." She disappeared into the kitchen to find something she could use for the flowers I'd brought.

Harrison patted the furry head of the stuffed animal. "I haven't needed one of these since forever ago."

"I can take him back if you want," I offered, knowing it had been a silly idea in the first place.

He hugged the bear to him and winced at the effort. "Not a chance. Yogi here will join little Boo Boo, the other one you got me at the hospital. Then all I need is a picnic basket full of food and it'll be a day of fun."

"We're also running out of space to put these on display," Azalea said, returning with the flowers hanging out of a crystal pitcher. "At least one of our wedding presents we've managed to open is being put to good use."

"Add it to the group on the table, babe. I won't be sitting up to eat there for a while," Harrison suggested. He shifted his position in the recliner and bit his lip to suppress a groan of pain. His hand shot to his left side.

Azalea set down the bouquet and rushed over to him. "I told you to ask for my help when you wanted to move."

He gripped her hand in his. "Honey, it's normal.

You were there when the doctor said it might take four to six weeks to get back to my usual routine. If I didn't die at the hospital after having two surgeries, internal bleeding, and a blood transfusion, then I'm not going to die here."

His wife knelt down by the chair and pressed her cheek against their clasped hands. "Don't even say something like that. Definitely not that word."

Petting her hair, Harrison comforted Azalea, taking on the role of caregiver even though he was still the recovering patient. My clenched stomach sided with her that he shouldn't talk about dying, but I kept that thought to myself. We'd come too close to losing him, so I sympathized with his new wife that talking about the horrific possibility of what could have happened still scared the pants off of us.

We'd stayed at the hospital off and on over the week and a half after the surgery, several of us taking turns to support Azalea and making sure she didn't run herself into the ground. With Gloria sick from whatever had hit her after the coven meeting, the girls and I played a bigger part in offering support. Since we weren't immediate family, we spent most of our time in the waiting room and rotated who would sit with the new wife in the room or bring her food and drink.

Ebonee had stepped in like a true leader, sustaining those of us on Team Azalea by bringing fresh clothes or better food than what they had at the hospital cafeteria. She'd checked in several times during each day on Harrison's status. Even after they'd stabilized him and we went on a rotating schedule for us to get the rest Azalea refused to do for herself, the head of the coven went above and beyond to stay informed and involved.

"Your standing there and staring at us is getting a little creepy, Rue. I know you must have something you want to talk to me about, and we might as well get it over with before you and my wife start planning my funeral." Harrison winked at me, but his joke fell flat for the rest of us girls in the room.

"I would punch you if I thought you could take it," his wife complained.

I crossed my arms. "You see how you're upsetting your wife, and it's definitely not fun to listen to you be so morbid. Promise me you'll stop doing it."

"Isn't it better if I joke about it rather than dwell on things?" he countered. "If I make light of it, then maybe it won't be so heavy."

Picking up the bag I'd set at my feet, I waved it in

the air to tempt him. "Promise or you won't get my real present for you."

He manhandled his new teddy bear. "You mean, Yogi wasn't the best thing?"

"I like stuffed animals just fine, but I figured you needed something a little more entertaining to help speed your recovery." The plastic bag crinkled in my hands as I shook it again. "But first, I want to hear your solemn oath."

"Me, too," echoed Azalea.

Harrison groaned in agitation. "Fine." Setting Yogi on the side table and holding up his right hand, he smirked. "I swear I won't say any words that convey the truth that I came pretty close to leaving this Earth, even though I think embracing that fact will help me appreciate every single second I get to live with my beautiful wife."

A little choked up at the spectacle of the newly-weds' love, I bit the inside of my cheek to keep from tearing up. "I guess that will do. Here, I saved this just for you."

He accepted the bag with curious thanks and pulled the plastic-covered item out. His eyes widened almost as big as his grin. "No way. Where in the world did you get this?"

"It looks like an old magazine. Why would you

want that?" Azalea wrinkled her nose at my perfect gift.

"Uh, honey, this is *The New Mutants #98.*" Harrison handled the gift with care, bringing it closer to his face to admire the artwork. "It's in incredible condition."

Azalea looked between her husband and me. "I don't get it."

"This is a collectible, and Ruby Mae must have found it through her family business. It could fetch well over a thousand dollars on the market in this kind of condition." He glanced up at me. "This is too much."

I blushed under his attention, pleased at my choice. "Naw, I figured someone who almost shook hands with the reaper deserved to get something he really wanted."

"Why does she get to make that joke and I can't?" Harrison complained, narrowing his eyes at me. "Although I really do want it, so I guess I'll let it slide. Thanks, Rue."

"Nope, I still don't get it, but if it makes you happy, then I second that." Azalea beamed at me. "Thanks, Ruby Mae. Can I get you some sweet tea or something? Why don't you sit down for a bit so you, too, can watch my sweet husband ignore us and drool all over his comic book while he reads it."

"Oh, no. I would never take it out to read. That would risk its value." He cradled the comic book to his chest, careful not to wrinkle a page while he loved on it.

"Read away, my friend. I'm glad I rescued it for you. Like you said, it's my job. And giving that to you is my absolute pleasure." I sat on the edge of the couch. "Actually, if you don't mind, I do have some questions to ask you if you're not in too much pain."

Azalea stayed next to her husband. "Are you sure you're not too exhausted?"

Harrison rolled his eyes and snorted. "Don't make me break my promise reminding you that I'm still here with all my parts functioning. We'll need a little more privacy if you need me to prove it to you. We never did get to go on our honeymoon." He wiggled his eyebrows at his wife.

She turned five shades of pink, dodging her eyes from me and giving him a playful smack. "You're out of luck, Mr. Dobbs. The doctor said it would be a good four to six weeks before you return to *any* normal activity."

"Challenge accepted, Mrs. Dobbs." Harrison ran the back of his hand down her cheek. "Have we made it too awkward for you, Rue, or do you still want to interrogate me?"

Their displays of affection did make me feel like an intruder, but I needed to hear his side of things before I left. "I'll get through this as quick as I can so you two can have some alone time. I guess the biggest thing I want to know is, what happened from your perspective?"

Harrison closed his eyes while he recounted his version of the event. "I was having so much fun dancing with all of y'all and really celebrating with those I knew cared about us the most. The band was playing their butts off."

"Yeah, Hunter and the boys are really good. I'm thinking they'll be getting offers sometime soon to move up to Nashville," I admitted. "But do you remember when you left? How did you end up in the darkened area behind the table you'd sat at for dinner?"

Harrison shrugged. "I had to go to the bathroom."

"So did I, but I didn't run into you when I went up to the house to use the restroom." Maybe we'd missed each other by mere moments in passing.

"Uh, I'm a guy. I didn't exactly need to go up to the house." Harrison shrugged at the truth. "Not to gross you two out. But now I'm wishing I had gone up to use the actual bathroom because maybe I wouldn't have put myself in danger." He reached out to take Azalea's hand, linking his fingers through hers.

My heart raced, preparing to ask the most important question. "Did you see who did it?"

His face dropped. "No. I wish with everything in me I had so I could tell that to the police. Maybe then they'd stop hounding me for my account. I know they think Azalea did it, but there's no way it was her."

"What do you remember about that moment?" I pressed, worried that I might be asking too much of my injured friend.

"I was taking care of business, and about the time I finished, I heard steps coming up from behind. I didn't turn around because I wanted to zip up my fly first and make myself presentable, just in case it was my wife." He stroked Azalea's hair. "But before I turned around, I felt a sharp pain in my left side and fell to the ground. Whoever it was took off without me being able to see who it was."

We were no closer to an answer than when he was unconscious at the hospital. "Do you think it was the footsteps of a guy or a girl?"

"I was a little too busy dealing with a knife

sticking into me and trying to breathe." He grimaced in pain and grunted at the memory.

Azalea stood up and shielded her husband from my view. "I think that's enough. He doesn't need to keep talking about it if he can't remember anything. I'm sorry, but I'm kicking you out, Ruby Mae."

My curiosity fizzled with the rise of guilt in my gut. "I completely understand, and I apologize if I went too far. Get some rest, both of you. I'll stop by another time, but just to make sure you two aren't trying to kill each other from boredom."

Harrison pointed at me in mock horror. "See, she did it again, making the same kind of joke. This feels totally unfair."

"You could give me back the comic book," I teased, snapping my fingers for it.

"Never mind," he replied with a wave to shoo me away. "Now, leave me to my girl and my gift."

I laughed, relieved at his lack of annoyance at me. "I'm not even going to ask which one you want to spend time with first. No need to get you even more injured." A thought popped in my head, and I risked pushing my two friends to the brink. "Wait, I have two more things and I swear I'll go away."

"Rue," Harrison warned.

"It's actually one question I want both of you to

answer. Can you remember what song was playing when you left the dance floor?" If they could come up with the correct tunes, it could narrow down exactly when Harrison was attacked.

They conferred with each other, suggesting and vetoing titles. "I think it was after that wagon wheel song because I like singing along so much that I waited to relieve myself until after it was finished," Harrison said.

I hadn't been there for that fun song, so already we could narrow down the time based on Mac's scheduled estimations. "Azalea?"

"I can't remember much other than throwing down as much as possible. We were also a little tipsy from drinking straight out of the bourbon bottle." She concentrated, biting her lip while reminiscing. "Although I do remember, it was a slow song because it took me a hot second to realize my new husband wasn't there to twirl me around."

Even without a specific title, it was something concrete I could work with. "That's when you left to go looking for him?"

Azalea tilted her head to the side. "Actually, no. I was going to go up to the house to use the bathroom, but I was told Harrison was waiting to see me."

My heart rate kicked into high gear, and I leaned

against the frame of the door to steady myself and stay upright. "Who told you?"

Azalea turned to Harrison, her mouth open with shock. "I didn't even think about it, I was so focused on what happened to you." She faced me again, her eyes glazed with burgeoning tears. "Gloria. It was Gloria who told me where I could find him."

CHAPTER THIRTEEN

My fist banged on the door to Gloria's place again. She hadn't answered the other twenty or so times I'd knocked, but I didn't know what else to do while waiting for her brother to meet me in her driveway. I considered messaging our mutual friends, but until I got a chance to talk to her in person, I thought it best to keep my gnawing fears to myself.

Wesley's car squealed around the corner, blowing through the stop sign. He pulled in right next to my truck and killed the engine, jumping out to join me. "Is she answering?" he asked, breathless and ashen.

"I figure she'd let me in if she was home. Since I can't get into the house, I can't see if her car's in the garage. I didn't know what else to do." I caught the neighbor across the street watching us. "Don't suppose you have a key to get us inside so Gladys Kravitz over there doesn't call the police on us?"

Wesley hopped down from the small brick patio by the door. "No, but I know where she hides the spare." He picked up a rock and brought it to his lips. "Hello, friend." After the sound of a slight click, he dumped a key out into his palm.

"Was that a *Lord of the Rings* reference?" I asked. "Why didn't you say the word in Elvish?"

He scrambled back up on the porch. "Because Glo and I loved those books growing up, and the movies were awesome. But I think learning a fictional language might have taken our fandom one step too far." With a turn of the spare key, he entered her small house. "Glo! Where are you?" he yelled out, tossing the key into a bowl sitting on the decorative table next to the door.

In all my years since I'd been friends with Gloria, I'd never known her to tolerate a whole lot of chaos. She'd rearrange her side of the tiki bar at least once a night to keep it tidy and efficient despite sometimes encroaching into my space. For the most part, I didn't care about her tidying tendencies. Seeing the state of her home ramped up my concern to another level.

Some crumpled tissues, a half-empty glass of water, and broken crackers littered the floor beside the living room couch. A crocheted blanket hung halfway off the cushions.

"Something's wrong," Wesley declared, picking up the multicolored throw. "She always gives me a hard time if I use it and don't fold it up and place it right here on the edge."

We inspected every room, not sure of what we should be looking for. The kitchen reflected the same level of disarray with boxes of food opened on the counter and dishes in the sink. My shoe stuck to something tacky on the floor that hadn't been wiped up after being spilled.

"I don't like this." Wesley left me, his footsteps pounding down the hallway. "Her bed's a mess," he called out from the back bedroom. "And there are clothes lying all over the place."

I passed the bathroom with a towel rumpled on the tile floor. Picking it up, my fingers tested the cloth. Not damp. "I don't think she's been here in at least the last few hours. When's the last time you talked to her?"

Wesley met me in the hall, his jaw tense with stress. "I talked to her yesterday morning and asked if she was feeling any better. It's not like her to be sick for an entire week. Or to come down with anything. Out of the two of us, she was the kid who never missed a day of school." He leaned against the wall and dialed her number on his phone.

Taking advantage of his moment of distraction, I entered her bedroom to see if there was anything a girlfriend might notice that a brother would miss. The drawer from her bedside table was pulled open, the contents from inside strewn about on the floor. Whatever she was looking for, she'd searched for it in a hurry. A collection of pens and pencils rested underneath a small lamp. I checked underneath some magazines and under the bed to see if I could find whatever she might have been writing on. No notebook or pad. Not even a scrap of paper where I could attempt the old pencil trick to shade indentations to find out what she'd been writing.

More crumpled tissues were scattered about on the floor despite the trash can being right next to the bed. I pulled the cover and tangled sheets back out of desperation to find any indication as to what had happened to Gloria. A worn stuffed rabbit wearing a green hat and holding what might have been the felt remnants of a faded carrot rolled into view.

With great care, I lifted the well-cared for item up and placed it on the wrinkled pillow. What nightmares or monsters were bothering her if she needed her bunny to hold while she slept? My instincts screamed at me that I already knew what the answer was, even without talking to her.

"I can't get through to Glo." Wesley joined me in the bedroom. "But her phone does ring instead of going straight to voicemail, which means she has it on. So, she has to know we're looking for her." He leaned his hands on the wooden dresser and stared into the mirror in front of him. In frustration, he swiped everything she had on top of the dresser onto the floor, shouting expletives.

I waited for his outburst to pass and his breathing to even out before attempting to speak. "That's not going to help, but I hope it felt good. Maybe you need to hold the bunny for a while for some comfort."

"What bunny?" he asked, turning around and perching on the edge of the dresser.

I pointed out the well-worn rabbit I'd set up on the pillow. "Mr. Hippity Hop over there."

Wesley spotted the stuffed animal and his anger vanished. He picked up the toy and held it in his hands. "You found Benjamin. At least that's what she named him after those British animal tales from that author with the weird name. I guess the rabbit in the books wore a green hat, so when she was given this, she named it after the character."

"That's sweet. I had a stuffed sheep that was white, but I called it Baa Baa Black Sheep after the lullaby." Feeling nostalgic, I tucked away the desire to ask Granny Jo if my old snuggle buddy was somewhere inside the big house.

"If she had Ben, then she must have been feeling pretty awful. He's usually somewhere in a box in her closet." Wesley put the rabbit back where I'd placed it. "Why didn't she tell me she wasn't doing well when I called her?"

"Are you saying you never came over the entire week she was sick?" I asked.

He rubbed the back of his neck. "I did bring her some takeout food, like a big container of egg drop soup and some fried rice from her favorite Chinese place. But I didn't do much more than meet her at the door." The springs of the mattress squeaked as Wesley slumped down on the bed. "I'm a horrible brother."

Choosing to comfort him rather than to ruin the moment rallying him into a frenzy to find Gloria, I sat next to him and patted his thigh. "No, you're not. You're incredibly busy because you work too much. You take as many shifts as you can at Ellie's Diner during the day, and then you work your butt off as a barback at the Tiki."

He hung his head. "You're right. I'm so exhausted, and I take it for granted that Gloria always has her life together since mine isn't."

I tapped his leg with a little more oomph. "Yeah, buddy, you're not in your early twenties anymore. Working all hours of the day and drinking part of your paychecks until late in the night isn't exactly healthy. Nor gonna attract a good woman."

He smirked. "I do okay."

"But wouldn't you like to find your own Azalea like Harrison did?" I pushed, standing up and maneuvering around a pile of clothes to get to the bathroom.

"Hey, are we going to make this about my love life or about discovering where Glo's gone?" Wesley deflected, following me.

I picked up a prescription bottle. "This says to take right before going to bed. It wasn't filled that long ago, but there aren't that many pills left in here." Shaking the orange plastic container, only a few white circles rattled around.

Her brother took the bottle from me and read the directions. "She hates these. Told me the make her sleepwalk and eat. I mean, maybe that's why things are so out of order in here. Because she's been taking the sleeping pills. But if that's the case, why did she feel she needed them?"

An alarming thought dawned on me. "She wouldn't drive after she took one, would she?"

Wesley tossed the bottle into the small sink and ran out of the master bedroom. My feet dragged a little as I trailed behind him, my fear becoming more palpable. What had Gloria done that had her acting so erratic? And if she'd run away, how far had she made it?

"Her car's gone." Wesley shouted after checking the garage. "I can only hope she wasn't under the influence of sleeping pills when she drove. But now I think we should alert the police."

The same thought had occurred to me too, but if the local authorities got involved, it would block my chance to find out the truth. After Azalea's revelation of how she ended up in the right place to find Harrison because of Gloria, I could only conclude the worst until I talked with my friend.

"I don't think that's a good idea, Wes." I put my hand over his phone to stop him from dialing.

"What do you mean? My sister is missing, and we need help tracking her down. The local police or county sheriffs can run her license plate and help." He pushed my hand off his.

Desperate to stop him, I blurted out the only thing I could think of. "It's possible Gloria is somehow involved with Harrison's stabbing. And that could be the reason things don't feel right and she's not here."

He stopped tapping the face of his phone. "What are you talking about?"

I held up my hands to get him to listen, telling him what Azalea told me. "If she wasn't directly involved, then she must have seen something. But that doesn't make sense either because why wouldn't she tell the authorities so the person who did it could be arrested for trying to hurt or even kill the husband of her best friend?"

Wesley backed away from me. "Nothing you're saying makes sense. My sister wouldn't hurt Harrison."

"I didn't say that she did necessarily," I countered in a weak defense.

"Oh, yes, you are." He stomped toward the front door. "Either you're saying my sister was in cahoots with someone who stabbed my best friend and she's covering for that person or you're saying she actually did the deed herself!" His voice echoed off the walls of the small house. "Either way, you're wrong."

I ran up behind him and slammed the front door shut, blocking his exit. "I hope I am, Wes. I really do. But until we're sure what's going on with her, I think it's risky to get law enforcement involved."

"You're making some huge leaps there, Rue. I know you fancy yourself some slick investigator, but you're not. You're a scrapheap scrounger, not a detective." He pushed me back and pulled the door open. "Stick to what you're good at and stay away from my sister." Taking one step out the door, he turned around with his eyes cast down. "In fact, don't come near either of us."

I couldn't watch as he pulled away, but I heard the squeal of his tires as he gunned his car down the road. My stomach dropped, and a wave of nausea hit me. I'd just insulted one of my oldest friends and implied his sister might have tried to murder his best friend. I'd gone off of nothing but my gut instinct and the slight mystery of how Gloria knew where Harrison had been stabbed. If I were him, I'd hate me, too, right about now.

Taking the key out of the nearby bowl, I left the house in the same condition we'd found it in and locked the door on my way out. Not wanting to leave the key where someone might find it, I pocketed it. My legs dragged like they were sunk into cement shoes as I walked to my truck. The curtain in the window across the street ruffled, and the same nosy woman from before stared back at me.

If I didn't doubt everything I'd just said, I might have gone over to ask her when the last time was she saw her neighbor coming or going. But since I'd put my foot so far into it with Wesley, the wind in my sails to find all the puzzle pieces and put them together died.

Giving up on my quest to find Gloria, I drove home and ignored the waves from my uncle, bypassing the barn and heading straight for my little cottage. With all of my clothes still on, I flopped into bed and pulled the quilt over my head, blocking out the rest of the world and hiding for as long as I could.

"GO AWAY," I MOANED, IRRITATED AT THE INCESSANT pounding that repeated over and over. Half asleep, I sat up and checked for the time.

It was almost a quarter past four, and since the entire room was bathed in darkness, it had to be in the early morning. I'd slept through the rest of the day and might have made it into the morning with the first full night's rest in a long time if it weren't for the wild knocking on my front door.

"If it's Luke, I'll kill him. Even if he's here to rub my feet," I muttered as I switched on the light and walked down the hallway. With a yawn, I scratched the top of my head and waddled with slow steps to torture whoever it was still banging. "I'll kill him, even though he's technically already dead."

Prepared to chew my boyfriend a new one for not calling first, I yanked the door open. "What do you think you're—"

"I'm sorry, Ruby Mae. You need to let me in, and I'll tell you everything." A very disheveled Gloria pushed past me and entered my house, unwilling to wait for my invitation or response.

CHAPTER FOURTEEN

We sat opposite each other, Gloria occupying the middle of my couch. I pulled my legs up underneath me as I settled into the overstuffed side chair, waiting for her to say something. Anything to explain her actions that had no plausible explanations.

She brushed her hair behind her ear, which didn't do much to help the tangled mess on her head except to get it out of her face. "I don't suppose you have anything I could eat?"

I expected a story about taking too many sleeping pills and finding herself in some strange scenario. A tiny part of me thought she might come right out and make a bold confession that she was the one who wielded the knife. Asking for food did not top the list of things I thought she'd might say.

"I don't think I have much, but we can see what's in my fridge." I abandoned the soft seat and shuffled into my kitchen, still unclear as to what was truly going on. Opening the refrigerator, I found very few things to offer. "I've been eating a lot up at the big house, so there's not much to choose from. I've got about one and a half spears of pickles swimming in juice. And there are two eggs left in this carton."

"Do you mind if I use those?" Her voice came from right beside my left shoulder, and I flinched away from her. "I haven't eaten since yesterday morning," she muttered in a low voice, her eyes downcast at the floor.

In a matter of minutes, I sat on top of a nearby counter, watching Gloria push the yellow goo around in a pan with a wooden utensil. Her hands shook as the liquid turned to small lumps of scrambled egg, and I wanted to ask how she'd gotten to this condition and why. But the girl deserved to refuel a little before being hit by a barrage of questions.

I slid off the counter and found a plate for her meager meal. "Here." The toaster dinged, and the last piece of bread popped up golden brown. "I think there's a little bit of butter left in the door of the fridge."

She scraped a knife across the toast over and over until the butter spread in a thin layer. Tearing it down the middle instead of cutting it in half, she used the bread to push the finished eggs onto the fork and dug in.

With loud noises of consumption, the small plate of food disappeared in a few bites. Figuring she would be done in less time if I didn't ask her questions, I distracted myself by filling two glasses with water and setting one down in front of her. My finger tapped on the counter, counting down the seconds until I could unleash my utter bewilderment on her.

Gloria dropped her fork with a clatter and took a couple of swallows of water. She wiped her mouth off with the back of her hand and gave me her full attention. "Thank you for that."

"Holy hexes, Gloria!" I yelled, unable to contain the explosion of frustration. "You've been MIA for who knows how long, and you're sitting there thanking me for a little bit of food when what you should be doing is telling me what in Hades is going on?" She shrank away from me and the volume of my outburst, and a little guilt seeped into my gut. I reached out to touch her arm, speaking in a more reasonable voice, "Seriously. What's going on?"

Pulling away from my touch and picking up the glass of water, she walked back to the couch. "I've been trying to figure that out for days now. One second, everything in my world was normal. Except for having to support my best friend whose husband got stabbed in the middle of the reception on their wedding night."

"It's been utterly surreal lately," I agreed, occupying the same seat as before, determined to stay close to her. "Your brother and I came over to your house to check on you, and it was an absolute mess."

She snorted once and leaned back against the cushions. Her finger pointed at her chest. "Then it matches what I feel in here. Ever since Crystal took me home, I've felt like something's not right. Like I was one of the eggs I just cooked, and somebody cracked me against something hard and all my insides got scrambled."

I'd assumed she'd gotten sick in some way with her extreme reaction after the ritual at the coven meeting. "I guess it wasn't bad chicken salad then?"

"That's what I thought at first. Well, that and talking to Azalea's parents. Every word her father uttered sliced right through me." She rubbed the spot over her heart. "And then after I got home, I gave it twenty-four hours for whatever it was to work through my system. Except it got worse instead of better. And then there were the hallucinations every time I tried to get a little rest."

I gripped the arm of the chair, my entire being on edge. "What hallucinations? I'll admit, we found the almost empty bottle of sleeping pills. And Benjamin."

At the mention of her stuffed animal, the haunted expression she wore eased with a slight grin before the shadowed pain returned. "I was willing to try anything and everything to make it all stop. Benjamin used to be able to chase away the monsters." She dashed a tear away with a shaky hand. "Too bad this time, I think I'm the one who's a monster."

I got up to grab a box of tissues while she fell apart on my couch. Despite my need to find out what she meant by those words, Gloria was still my friend who needed help. The least I could do was give her my patience. And some tissues she could snot on.

Setting the box on the coffee table, I took a seat right next to her on the couch and put my arm around her shoulders. "Sometimes if we tell someone else about what's scaring us, the monsters will go away." I heard my father's voice in my words, and I silently thanked him for his affectionate way of taking care of me all by himself while I grew up.

Gloria blew her nose and crumpled up the used tissue. "I don't think it will change things. I kept trying to deny what I saw in here," she said, tapping the side of her head. "But it's all too real when I close my eyes. And it fills in the blanks like I'm the missing puzzle piece." Her voice wavered as she kept talking.

Exchanging the used tissue for a new one, I turned to face her. "Then let me see if I can guess what you're avoiding telling me. I talked to Harrison and Azalea yesterday."

Startled out of her misery, Gloria grabbed my hands. "Then he's okay?"

I rubbed my thumbs in circles on her skin, trying to chase away her nervous tremors. "He's recovering. Back to joking around. Azalea's hovering over him like he could disappear in front of her eyes."

At the mention of her best friend, Gloria broke down again into hysterics. "I would have gone over to see them. I wanted to. But..." she trailed off, her body racked from a bone-deep bawling.

I stopped stroking her hand. "Honey, Azalea recalled something that has me a little worried, but it might explain your hallucinations." As much as I cared for my friend, I needed to get to the heart of the truth. "When I asked her how she'd found Harrison when she did, she said that it was you who told her where to find him."

She rocked forward and held her head in her hands. "Then it's true," she murmured.

If she was confessing what I thought she was, a part of me wanted to scramble away from her. But the wreck of a person sitting on my couch wasn't capable of hurting me in her current state. Caught in limbo between wanting to comfort her and wondering if I should be calling the authorities, I compromised and patted her back, allowing myself to scoot just a couple of inches away.

"What's true?" I pushed.

She lifted her head and held her dominant hand out in front of her, staring at it like it wasn't her own appendage attached to her body. "I stabbed Harrison."

My pulse raced and my flight instinct kicked into high gear, but I forced myself to stay put and see this through. "Are you sure?"

Gloria sniffed hard and wiped her nose with her other arm. "Yeah. I'm sure. I'm the puzzle piece that completes the picture."

I'd expected to gloat in victory when I uncovered the person who stabbed Harrison. Instead, I struggled to keep the wave of nausea at bay. Pushing off of the couch, I paced in front of her. "Why did you come here tonight?"

She moaned low and long and sat up straighter. "I think I needed someone I knew cared about me to find out the truth and actually execute the one thing I haven't been able to make myself do." Pleading with her eyes, she clasped her hands together as if begging. "You have to turn me in."

It was the logical conclusion to the investigation. My spell phone still sat on the table next to my bed, but I couldn't bring myself to fetch it and be the one who turned in my friend, no matter what she'd told me. "And what am I supposed to say? Hi, this is my friend Gloria, and she thinks she stabbed her best friend's new husband. No, there's no concrete evidence, just some visions." Someone like Deputy Sheriff Caine might jump at the chance based on less than circumstantial evidence, but I wasn't willing to make the call just yet.

Gloria shrank into herself, her wits coming very close to their jangling end. "Then what am I supposed to do?"

A rooster crowed off in the distance, and the

natural alarm awoke a new idea. "Come on, get off the couch."

"Are you going to turn me in?" she asked, a little hope and fear mixed in her tone. "I deserve to be locked up if it all really happened."

Grasping her hands, I pulled on her until she stood. "I'm not your judge nor your jury. And I'm not making any promises as to whether or not law enforcement will have to get involved. But there's somewhere I want to take you first to have you checked out."

I escorted her out of my house and found her car door wide open with the light from the inside piercing the early morning. A repeating ding meant her key was still in the ignition, and I supported Gloria to the passenger side and settled her into the seat.

"Where are we going?" she asked as I got into the driver's side.

"To see a healer and get a second opinion."

CHAPTER FIFTEEN

Gloria tucked into a plate of more eggs, a drop biscuit, and some fried-up country ham while seated at our family dinner table. My ghostly great-grandmother and I kept a close watch while she devoured everything like she hadn't seen food in a couple of days.

"That girl was running on empty. No wonder she's a little touched in the head at the moment," Granny Jo stared at my friend with a mix of sympathy and wariness.

"What do you think? Am I right that something is wrong with her?" I asked in a low whisper. Making a risky decision I might pay for later, I had withheld my friend's confession from Granny in order to keep her from being too biased with her estimations.

My great-grandmother harrumphed, and her corporeal figure shimmered in and out of focus. "I think you're keeping something back from me because that girl there," she pointed a bony see-through finger at Gloria, "is a walking, talking threat, and you brought her right up into our house."

I waved my hands back and forth in protest. "No, I don't think she'll go picking up a knife to hurt one of us." The second the words popped out of my mouth, I regretted them.

Granny Jo's eyes bugged out of her skull. "So, that's what this is about. You brought a child who's practically smothered in unstable magic here because she's done something wrong, haven't you?" She didn't wait for me to confirm her suspicions. "I could scold you seven ways to Sunday, but that won't change that there's a body hurtin' in my presence and I'm not doing anything about it. Go upstairs to my room and fetch me that black leather bag that's stashed underneath my side of the bed. And then check the pantry and grab a couple bundles of smudging sticks."

"Thanks, Granny," I uttered in relief.

She shook her head. "Don't thank me yet. I may have been a strong healer in life, but I'm a little limited in death."

A mass of spectral energy and a few blobs of spirits clustered around the bottom of the stairs. Holding my breath, I pushed through the remnants of my departed family to retrieve what my great-grandmother wanted.

Her room remained exactly as it had been after she'd passed. The quilt she'd made for her wedding night still covered the double bed. A fine layer of dust coated the furniture and all the items lying around, as if nobody lived in there. Which was technically true. I'd have to remember to come in and clean sometime soon. Kneeling down on the wooden floor by the right side of the bed, I lifted the lacy dust ruffle out of the way and strained to spot the bag.

"What are you doing in here, Ruby Mae," my father interrupted from the doorway. "It's barely past five in the morning. And why do I smell bacon?"

My heart raced from being startled, but I stayed focused on my task, spellcasting a small ball of light. The bag lay a little out of my reach, and I laid all the way down on the floor, stretching to grab it. "I've got a problem and Granny's helping me with it," I said, my fingertips brushing against the leather.

"Here. Let me reach it." Dad waited for me to scoot out of the way before crouching and reaching his long arms underneath. He dragged out the satchel but wouldn't hand it over. "Before I give this to you, tell me what's going on."

His stern expression left me no room to hold anything back, so with quick words and a few breaths, I filled him in.

"You think Gloria's the one who stabbed Harrison?" he asked. "If that's true, why is she here in the house and not down at the police station?"

"She came to me for help, and I don't think she did anything on purpose. Plus, there's not a whole lot of evidence from someone who says they've had hallucinations that make them think they committed a crime," I defended. "I thought that maybe Granny could prove that something else is going on." I held out my hand to accept the requested bag.

"I'll take it," he insisted, shifting it into his other hand and gripping my shoulder. "But I need you to understand something and make me a promise. If your great-grandmother and I think she's involved in any real way, you will involve the police without any questions."

I nodded, unable to give voice to a promise I didn't know if I could keep.

He lifted an eyebrow of suspicion but waited at the door for me to exit first. While Dad took the bag into the living room, I went to the pantry to retrieve the sage.

Dried herbs hung from the ceiling in the small room stacked with canned and dried goods. Mason jars of various herbs and unlabeled mixes sat on a couple of shelves. I pulled down a small cardboard box with no lid and picked out a couple of tied bundles of sage from the large pile next to some loose dried herbs and some twine. About three or four times a year, we used them to cleanse the house and the rest of the property of any bad energy. Before I put the box back on the shelf, I thought better of it and took the whole thing with me just in case.

At his grandmother's bidding, Dad pulled out items from the bag and set them on the coffee table. Gloria sat on a wooden chair in the middle of the living room with her hands in her lap and her right leg bouncing with nerves, and my concern for her overwhelmed me.

Dani shuffled down the stairs in her bathrobe and pajamas to find me staring at our friend. "What's going on?" she yawned, wiping the sleep out of her eyes.

If everyone kept asking me the question, I'd spend more time giving explanations rather than helping. "Just get in here and help me assist Granny."

"I'm supposed to go meet Mom at the cafe to help out in about thirty minutes." She gazed at Gloria with sympathy. "But I heard the commotion and had to come see what's going on."

I breathed out a sigh. "It's a long story."

My cousin kissed me on the cheek. "And one that will probably end in you helping your friend at whatever cost like you always do. You want me to stay?"

I opened my mouth to tell her to go ahead, but her warm affection bolstered me and lessened my general worries. "Actually, yeah. It would be good to have you here, especially if things go wrong."

"I'll call Mom and then come join you," she agreed.

As she scampered up the stairs, I called out to her, "Try not to wake up your dad." Although Uncle Jo and his experiences could be useful at times, sometimes he could be like a bull in a china shop, and we needed a more delicate approach with Gloria.

A loud snore echoed through the second-floor hallway. Dani giggled. "Don't worry. He's a hard sleeper." She scampered upstairs.

"Child, you gonna bring me that box you're holding or what?" Granny Jo hollered at me.

"Yes, ma'am." I hurried my behind into the living room and tipped the container for her to see.

"Hmm," she deliberated. "I'd usually go with just some white sage, but let's add some Amaranth and thyme in as well. And maybe a sprig of lavender."

I did as she asked, picking through the herbs with care. "Which one's Amaranth?"

Granny Jo finished instructing my father in setting up crystals around the chair. She pointed into the box, "The one with the copper tufts of seeds. We'll need that to help unblock her mind and hopefully help her mend a little."

While I tied the herbs together, Dani joined us in some regular clothes. She retrieved a large amethyst crystal from inside the bag and gave it to Gloria to hold in her lap.

"Take that vial of golden liquid over there, Ruby Mae," Granny requested. When I obeyed, she continued. "If you wouldn't mind, could you warm the contents of it up a little?"

Calling on my magic, I sent a little heat into my palm, letting it radiate through my fingers. "Exactly how warm do you want it?"

"That should be enough. No need to scald her

with burning oil." My great-grandmother's figure inspected all of the elements we'd put together. "I'd do this myself, but if I'm going to observe how she reacts, I need you to act as my hands. Now, if you would, pour a little oil onto your fingertips and draw a cross on top of her forehead."

Gloria didn't flinch when the warm oil touched her skin. "What's that going to do?"

"It's frankincense. I'm hoping it will help calm you a little, child." She attempted to ease my friend's worries with a smile, but the crease in her brow conveyed her own concerns. "Buckley, after you open that window over there, I want you to take your place nearby with that black tourmaline like we talked about."

"Yes'm." My father opened the two windows of the room and a fresh breeze billowed the gauzy curtains.

"Danielle Josephine, I want you to find the large smoky quartz I got wrapped up in my bag and hold onto it on her other side," Granny Jo instructed. When she recognized the fear in Gloria's widened eyes, she floated in front of her, her hands reaching out as if she could touch my friend. "Don't you worry none, sweet girl. I'm just taking some precautions to protect all of us if something goes wrong."

"I hope it doesn't." Gloria's voice shook with uncertainty.

"Take a few deep breaths and let them in and out to ready yourself." My great-grandmother hovered away to give the rest of us room to move as she ordered. "Ruby Mae, if you would light that stick, we can get started."

Placing my fingertips on the end of the bundle of herbs, I concentrated until smoke rose in the air and a small spark kindled under my touch. I made sure it was lit well before blowing it out, watching the smoke curl. Granny Jo observed me with great scrutiny while I started from the top of her head and encircled Gloria with the spicy with a hint of sweet vapor.

In a steady voice, my ghostly great-grandmother started the ritual. "When you're ready, take in a really deep breath and close your eyes for me."

For a cleansing, we usually repeated the steps seven times. But by the second circling, a slight sheen of a murky substance manifested on Gloria's skin. It wrapped around her like sickly ribbons that undulated with life, although half of them hung in shredded tatters. "What is that?"

Gloria's eyes popped open. "What?" She fidgeted in her seat with renewed fear. "It's all over me."

"It's best if you don't look, child. We're doing the best we can, but your squirming could make things worse," warned my great-grandmother.

"Should I stop?" I asked, worried at my close proximity to whatever it was enveloping my friend.

"No, keep going. Let's see if smudging her will make things better." Granny Jo paused. "But just in case, Buckley, why don't you and your niece go ahead and place the stones around the chair. I'd rather be prepared than sorry."

My muscles tensed with anxiety, but I continued to wave the bundle of herbs and waft the smoke against Gloria's body. Some of the murky ribbons untied and disappeared, but others drew in a little tighter. My friend whimpered, and a bead of sweat dripped down the side of her face.

"I think I'm going to throw up," Gloria announced, giving us as much warning as she could.

Granny Jo held up her hands. "Then let's stop. I'm not sure if we're doing you more harm than good anyway. The bathroom's around the corner and on your left."

My friend leapt off the chair, covering her mouth with her hands. Dani followed her to help, leaving me with my father and his grandmother.

Dad sat down on the edge of the coffee table. "This isn't working."

"If I had proper use of my body and could do things for myself, I might have been able to do more. But I can't guarantee anybody's safety." Her figure wavered with her disappointment. "And as much as I love your big heart, Ruby Mae, I won't risk our family."

I nodded, keeping my eyes on the floor so she didn't mistake my frustration in the situation as anger with her. "What were those things wrapped around her?" I asked.

Dad exchanged a knowing glance with our ghostly kin. "Nothing good. By my guess, someone has spellbound her."

"And did a shoddy job of it, too," Granny agreed. "I thought it was her own magic gone awry. Whoever spellcast it must be pretty powerful. Or pretty dumb. Either way, she needs more help than we can give her."

"We need a skilled healer," Dad suggested. "Like the one who helped you recover, butter bean. If you know how to reach her, I would call her right now."

Bringing someone else into the fold would mean one more person who would put everything together and possibly report Gloria to the authorities. I accepted that might be the final outcome no matter what, but the whole situation required someone with more experience or who wasn't a ghost of her former self in the truest sense.

"I think in order to have Dr. Tomasi keep things confidential, I'm going to have to bring in someone with a lot more finesse than me." I glanced between my father and my great-grandmother with regret, having kept my bargain with the coven leader a secret from them. "I'll call Ebonee and have her bring the healer with her."

Dani joined us. "I think you should call Wesley, too. At least someone from her family should be here with her."

THE RAYS OF DAYLIGHT SHONE THROUGH THE windows of the house. Our living room burst with all the extra people. Wesley ignored me, concentrating on staying by his sister's side while Dr. Beverly Tomasi executed a more thorough examination.

"You did good to reveal the bad energy through your work, Ms. Jewell," she complimented my great-grandmother. "And I think you made the right call if you couldn't be the one executing all the steps." She brushed her fingers over the oil on Gloria's forehead and sniffed them.

"That's frankincense," I interjected, struggling to stay silent on the sidelines.

"Nobody asked you," Wesley grumbled with agitation.

His sister scolded, "Don't take your anger at me out on Ruby Mae. I'm the one who came to her. Not the other way around."

He crossed his arms. "Still. I don't know why she or her family are even involved." Kneeling next to Gloria, he had a hard time obeying the edict from the doctor not to touch his sister. "If you had said something right away, I could have gotten you help sooner."

"I'm getting help now," Gloria insisted.

Ebonee took a step closer. "Beverly, what's your initial prognosis? She seems a little shaken but not in danger."

"You haven't seen what we have yet," I warned.

The doctor and healer patted Gloria on her knee and stood. "Based on what they told us, I think their initial assessment is probably right. I've never seen a case myself, but I read about it in my studies.

Someone probably spellbound her and not with very much care for the outcome."

The coven leader frowned. "Without solid proof, I don't know what to do."

"I didn't say I couldn't show you." The doctor picked her own larger bag off the floor and placed it next to Granny's. After rummaging through it, she took out a small ceremonial metal bowl and a bottle of amber liquid. She poured out some of the contents into the dish. "Can someone take this into the kitchen and heat it up?"

"I can do it," I volunteered. Taking the bowl from her, I summoned more heat into my palms. After a few quick moments, I gave it back. "If you need it hotter, let me know."

She thanked me and tipped her head in appreciation. Instructing Gloria to hold the bowl and breathe in the fumes, Dr. Tomasi took a spray bottle and misted the air around her. "Now, I'd like for you to repeat again what you think happened. What is it you've been seeing?"

Wesley got as close as he could to his sister, biting his thumbnail to keep from touching her. "I'm right here, Glo."

"I started seeing the same thing over and over

again after that coven meeting." Gloria closed her eyes and drew in a long breath over the contents of the bowl. "I'm on the dance floor, and I see Harrison leave the group. I feel compelled to follow him because I have to or else my whole world will fall apart."

Around her body, the same dark ribbons emerged, writhing and wriggling. Ebonee emitted an audible gasp, and my father restrained Wesley from stopping the proceedings.

Oblivious to our reactions, Gloria shifted in the seat. "It's dark wherever he went, and I approach him. But instead of calling out his name or saying anything, I plunge what's in my hand into his back."

She lunged forward with her hand out in front of her, and the bowl almost fell out of her lap. Wesley yanked free and crawled closer, but Ebonee's stern warning stopped him from interfering. The murky ribbons grew stronger in visibility the more she revealed.

"He falls down and I run," continued Gloria. "But as soon as I see Azalea, I'm torn apart inside. I tell my best friend where to find her husband so he won't be all alone." She opened her eyes, the last bit of her control evaporating into tears. "I don't know why I can see all that now, and I wish with everything in me it's not true."

"I understand," the doctor replied.

Glancing down, Gloria saw the binding magic surrounding her for the first time. With a yelp, she clawed at her body as if trying to tear it all away. "Wes, get it off of me!"

A new voice cut through the tension of the room. "I would advise no one but the doctor goes near her," Lieutenant Alwin stated.

"You just let yourself into our home?" Dad asked, his eyes finding mine. In all of the chaos, I'd forgotten to reset the wards to the house. "Isn't that unlawful?"

Ebonee raised her hand. "I asked her to come, Buck. Based on what I was told over the phone, I don't see how someone in law enforcement isn't involved. And since she's a higher-ranking warden as well, Olivia might be able to at least advise us."

He protested, "But she's on Jewell land. You know there are restrictions—"

Dr. Tomasi restrained Gloria's arms with the help of Wesley. "If you're not here to help, then take your argument to another room." Struggling to control her patient's squirming, she grunted at my great-grandmother. "Ms. Jewell, if you would stick around, I'm sure I could use your expertise."

Granny Jo disappeared and materialized in

between the trio of my father, the lieutenant, and Ebonee. "You three, take this to the kitchen. Dani Jo, you go on and help your mother out at the cafe. And Ruby Mae, you've done as much as you can. I love you, darlin', but leave us to do the rest."

"Thank you, Ms. Jewell." The doctor nodded at her fellow healer.

"Call me Josephine," my great-granny insisted.

Without a clear plan of what else I could do, I headed to the kitchen as well. The three other adults bantered back and forth over authority and what to do next. While they argued, I fetched a glass from the cupboard and the pitcher of sweet tea out of the fridge.

"Why don't you pour some for all of us? I'm afraid I was too stuck in my thoughts to offer. I apologize, ladies," Dad said, getting up to get three more glasses and set them on the table.

"It's fine, Buck. This has been a strange beginning to the day for all of us," Ebonee admitted, leaning forward to rest her elbows on the table. She moved back a little when I served her iced tea.

Feeling like an outsider to the three adults who held different levels of authority, I hopped up on the counter. "I can't work out what would be the next steps. I mean, are you here to arrest her, Lieutenant Alwin?"

"Actually, Miss Jewell, from my understanding, I don't hold any authority over what happens here on your property as part of the county sheriff's department," the lieutenant explained. "Whether it was intentional or not, your friend picked the right place to come to for sanctuary. And I offer my apologies to you, Mr. Jewell. I shouldn't have entered your domicile without your permission."

Dad considered her words with care and nodded. "Apology accepted."

My mind reeled trying to figure out how we'd come to this peculiar moment. "What exactly does it mean if Gloria's spellbound? I'm still unclear about that."

Ebonee leaned back in her chair, oddly comfortable and at ease in yoga pants and a comfort-fit top instead of her usual tailored outfit. "It's not something that's easily executed. Magic of that caliber has to have someone of rare magic spellcasting it. And given that it was done with sinister intent, whoever did this won't be doing well themselves."

My father set down his glass after taking a drink. "It's like I've always told you, butter bean. Magic has consequences."

The lieutenant stared into the sweet tea. "I hate to disagree, but you're not totally correct, Ebonee. Any witch who can wield magic can technically spellbind someone. And based on what you told me before I arrived and what I witnessed, this was far from a well-executed spell. I might even venture to guess whoever did it is pretty incompetent."

I considered their words carefully. "How could something like this happen? I mean, Gloria was acting completely fine leading up to the wedding. Even after, when she was supporting Azalea every day in the hospital, she didn't remember anything."

"I think Beverly can tell us more when she's finished, but my guess is that something triggered the spell the night of the wedding." Ebonee tapped the wooden table with a manicured nail for emphasis. "And if Olivia's right and the binding wasn't perfect, then she snapped herself out of it until the energy we shared at the end of the meeting ritual stripped whatever internal dam was holding the magic at bay."

"Like I said," added the lieutenant. "She was actually smart coming to you. If she'd been left on her own much longer, she might have done irreparable damage to herself or even others if things got even more out of control."

Her words eased a little of my guilt that the final outcome might be that Gloria had to be arrested and taken away.

Granny Jo's head poked through the far wall. "Y'all can come back now."

We found Gloria prostrate on the couch with Wesley cradling her head. The doctor continued to clean up and put things back into her bag while she talked to us. "I've given her a sedative to keep her calm since it seems the bindings are reacting to her emotions."

"What's your final assessment, Beverly?" Ebonee pushed.

The healer wiped her hands on a nearby towel and glanced between the coven leader and the lieutenant. "I'm not prepared to make an official statement. But off the record, I'd say she's not making this up. I think someone placed a spell on her that made her do things she wouldn't normally do."

"My sister would never knowingly stab Harrison," Wesley spit out, every muscle in his body tensing as if ready to fight. "You can't hold her responsible for something someone else made her do."

Lieutenant Alwin stepped in front of all of us. "I think it's best if I take her with me."

Gloria's brother and I both erupted into arguments. "I thought you couldn't arrest her because you're on our property," I pointed out, grasping onto any straw.

"As a county sheriff, she doesn't have the jurisdiction to apprehend Gloria. But as a district warden, she has free reign to do what she thinks needs to be done," Ebonee warned me, her voice low and even. "And I agree. I think it is for the best."

"You can't take her. I won't let you," Wesley threatened.

Dad moved between the coven leader and me in case things went sideways. "Take it easy, son, and listen first."

"I'm not your son." Gloria's brother balled his hand into a fist.

"That's enough," insisted the lieutenant. "I'm not doing anything official with your sister. No arrest either through mortal or magical institutions unless you choose to attack us. If I take her with me under warden protection, we can get her better care to try and free her from being spellbound."

"So, she won't be arrested?" Wesley clarified. "I'm not letting you take her now only to find out she's been put in jail."

My father shifted to face the lieutenant. "If all

you're doing is sheltering her at a warden facility, then maybe he can go along with you. That way, he'll better understand your intentions and how it'll help his sister."

"That sounds reasonable," Ebonee agreed. "I'd like to accompany you as well as a coven representative."

Lieutenant Alwin nodded once. "I'll wait in my vehicle outside." She left, and the air seemed easier to breathe in her absence.

Wesley cupped Gloria's cheek in his hand. "You okay with this, Glo?"

She blinked her eyes open. "I think it will be best. Then if anything truly bad happens, I won't hurt anybody else."

"Let me help you." Dad scooped the girl up in his arms to allow her brother to stand. "Here you go." He handed Gloria off to Wesley.

She threw her arms around her brother's neck and snuggled into his chest like the little girl who needed a tiny stuffed bunny named Benjamin. My heart clenched as they walked past me on their way to a warden facility. "For what it's worth, I'm sorry, Wes."

He stopped before walking out the door and spoke over his shoulder. "I won't lie and tell you I'm happy about this. But I think I might have to thank you in the long run if this all works out." He slowed down to make sure he didn't hit Gloria's head on the way out and disappeared.

Ebonee slung her purse over her shoulder. "I'm impressed that you held up your end of our agreement by bringing me in. It's a good step on your end of solidifying your place in the coven."

I followed behind her to the front door. "That's not why I did it."

"I know, which is what makes your actions even more noble. It seems the apple doesn't fall too far from the Jewell family tree." She tipped her head at my father and took her leave.

Granny Jo floated beside my father. "I still dislike her."

"Hmm." Dad kept his judgment to himself.

"How about I whip up some breakfast?" she offered, happy to do something more normal. "With all the stomachs rumbling in that room, I thought a storm was a-brewin'."

A storm was coming, but its fury would be aimed at whoever set everything in motion. "You know, Dad, there is one good thing that I learned."

"What's that, butter bean?" He placed his arm around my shoulders and squeezed.

I stared out the front door at the day just getting started. "Because the person who created the spell wasn't careful, Gloria only wounded Harrison, instead of killing him."

"True." Dad kissed the top of my head. "We can all be grateful for that."

"But there's one more thing," I continued with gleeful hope blooming in my chest. "If they're so inept that the magic didn't even work properly, then whoever they are, they've made it easier for me to catch them."

CHAPTER SIXTEEN

E xhaustion hit me after I ate my fill of breakfast. With all of the stress of the efforts made to help Gloria plus my ever-growing lack of sleep, I had a hard time figuring out how to even start narrowing down where to find the witch responsible.

"Maybe you should take a nap, butter bean," Dad suggested, peering over my shoulder at the few scribblings I'd scratched out on a piece of paper. "You look plum tuckered out. A little rest should do you good."

"I guess," I mumbled, doodling a cloud with lightning shooting from it.

He kissed the top of my head. "Stop being so hard on yourself. You did good this morning. It was tiring for all of us. Heck, even your great-granny's taking a break, and she's not even alive."

Although my ghostly great-grandmother's strong manifesting powers allowed her to appear more often than the other ghosts in the house, she had her limits. Involving her as much as we did this morning meant she needed to stay incorporeal to replenish her reserves. I wanted to get her thoughts on how spellbinding worked, but she'd used up the rest of her energy making us breakfast.

I yawned, rubbing my eyes. "I know. Sleep has been challenging for me ever since the night of the reception. I can't believe that was more than two weeks ago."

"Want to go up and take a nap in my bed?" he offered. "I've got to go over to Smooter to inspect and maybe purchase a collection of hand-punched pie tin safes. The dealer's retiring, and if he's willing to make me a deal for the whole bunch, we'll get some nice editions to sell. And I've been invited over for sweet tea and cookies by Ethel, Gladys, and Myrna."

Thinking of the infamous Thirsty Three who had a little crush on my father cheered me up. "That means you won't be getting home until much later because they'll chat you up and then convince you to stay for supper because you're too much of a Southern gentleman to turn down their kind offer."

"It means your father still has a little pep in his step." He winked at me, and I made a face at him.

"Yeah, to flirt with a bunch of old ladies. Way to go, Dad!" I shot him two thumbs up. "You know, one of these days, you should really try getting out there and dating someone closer to your age."

My father twisted the gold ring he still wore on his left hand. "I'd like to tell you not to bother me about that like I always do, but you know what? I've been thinking about that lately. Maybe I should at least try."

My eyebrows crawled into my hairline, and I bolted out of my chair. "Really?" I squealed, running up to him and almost jumping up and down with glee. "When you get back, we can sign you up for dating online and you can start looking at potential candidates."

He frowned again. "Can't I just go out and meet them like I used to?"

"This is the twenty-first century, Dad. You usually get to go through a list of candidates online first before you even see each other in person." Although he carried a spell phone with him, I never could get him to update to the latest model. "We can do it together if you like."

His face dropped with doubt. "Sounds like too much work to me."

I grabbed his hands. "Oh, don't give up so quickly. If you want to do it the old-fashioned way, we can go out to the Watering Hole."

Uncle Jo stomped into the kitchen, wiping his face off with a handkerchief. "Did somebody say the name of my favorite place other than here?"

"Dad says he might consider dating again," I exclaimed, hopping between my father and his brother.

"It's about time, Buck. I've been tellin' you for ages to dust yourself off and stop acting like you're already one of the ghosts that hasn't a lick of sense to move on after death." My uncle opened the refrigerator and pulled out a hunk of ham from last night's dinner. "If you want, I'll be your wingman."

"Like that's supposed to make me feel better. Remember the last girl you tried to hook me up with?" Dad asked. "It didn't end so well."

I quieted down. "Who? Mom?"

My father chucked me under the chin. "No, butter bean. This was right after your mama left us and I was feeling some kinda way. Your auntie stayed home with you and let the two of us go out to blow off some steam. The woman your uncle tried to set me up with wasn't exactly free to date."

Uncle Jo whipped off his trucker hat and scratched his bald head. "Yeah, you ended up with a mighty shiner and swore it was karma for cheating on your own wife."

My head bounced back and forth between the two brothers. "Just how old was I at the time?"

"Let's see. Dani Jo had just started kindergarten, so she was five," Uncle Jo mused.

"That would have made me around seven." My mother must have just left my dad and me when this happened. I went over to my father and wrapped my arms around his waist. "Sometimes I forget how tough you had it."

Dad embraced me and rocked me back and forth. "Don't you go thinking I resented you, butter bean. You're the absolute joy of my life. What happened between your mother and me, well, I never meant for it to splash onto you."

I lifted my face to gaze at his. So many people would tell me I looked like the spitting image of my mom when I was growing up. With flaming red hair like ours, it was hard for them not to make the comparison. But beyond sharing my father's eyes without the wrinkles, I knew I resembled him more than anyone else saw.

"I keep telling you this, old man," I teased, pinching his arm. "You deserve happiness, too. And whether you want me or your brother to be your backup, it'll warm my heart to see you take that first step to grab it."

Uncle Jo finished carving off slices of ham and put the dish back in the fridge. "It's getting a might bit too mushy in here. Don't you have an appointment to keep in Smooter?"

In a role reversal, I slapped my father's behind like he usually did to me. "Tell the Thirsty Three I said hey. And bring me back some pickled okra."

Knowing Gloria might be gone for a while, I drove her car back to my place to park it until she needed it again or her brother wanted it returned to her garage. Our barn cat waited by my front door to greet me, meowing and pacing as soon as he saw me.

"What's wrong, Buddy? Why are you all the way back here instead of at your normal spot?" I picked him up in my arms and noticed some light red streaks across his nose. "Has Rex been giving you a hard time?"

He rubbed his head underneath my chin and purred. Normally, I'd fix him a bowl of tuna or whatever I had that he might eat and bring it to him outside. But his warm fur and the slight rumble of his pleasure comforted me.

"Tell you what. I'll let you come in and take a break from that big bad rooster." I kissed his little mustached head and set him down, closing the front door behind us.

He wrapped himself around my ankles, his tail curling around my legs. With short mewls, he demanded to be picked up again, and I found it impossible to deny his request.

"Fine, you big baby. You can come nap with me on one condition." I scratched behind his ears, enjoying the increased volume of his purrs. "You keep your fleas to yourself."

DEEP SLEEP CONTINUED TO ELUDE ME, AND I TURNED over to my other side, spooning Buddy, whose little paws beat in the air while he dreamt of chasing mice. My mind raced to process everything that had happened so far and tried to prepare itself for what would come.

Now that the mystery of who did the stabbing had been discovered, another hole presented itself.

This morning, everyone kept using the term *spellbound*, but it did seem there was a general lack of understanding of exactly how any witch could pull that off. Granny Jo might know a little as did the lieutenant. But if I wanted to get a clearer picture of how whoever it was pulled it off, I needed to understand the act of spellbinding in the first place.

Careful not to disturb Buddy, I rolled out of bed and grabbed my spell phone. Scrolling through the contacts, I found the one person who I'd already called on once today. The line rang, and my stomach clenched in anticipation.

"This is Ebonee Johnson," the coven leader answered.

My voice caught in my throat, and I stuttered to speak.

"Who is this?" she demanded. I pictured her stony stare on the other end.

"It's Ruby Mae Jewell, ma'am."

A sharp sigh echoed in my ear. "We've barely gotten your friend settled, so I don't know why you're checking in on us."

I paced across my kitchen floor. "No, that's not why I'm calling. I wanted to ask you where I could find out more about how one of us could make someone be spellbound. Is there someone who's an expert on it that I can talk to?"

"There are many experts," she said with a sniff. "But none of them are in our immediate vicinity. However, I see the value in what you're asking, and if you're serious about putting in the work, then I can give you access to the coven's library."

I didn't even know the coven had a library. Then again, I'd barely been a member long enough to have explored all of the building other than knowing where the bathroom was and having sat like a schoolgirl in the leader's office.

Looking down at my disheveled appearance, I calculated how long it would take me to get ready. "I could meet you there in about forty-five minutes."

I listened to Ebonee talking to someone else on her side and excuse herself. Her steps echoed on the floor as she walked somewhere else. "I will be occupied here for longer than I anticipated. And I'd prefer if other members did not see what you were searching for and get curious. Rumors can have a more damaging effect than the truth sometimes. I think you'd agree it's better we keep things as quiet as possible."

"Y-e-a-h," I drew out. "About that. I was

wondering if I could bring some additional help to get through things a little quicker."

Even without seeing her, I knew I was testing Ebonee's patience. "As long as they're coven members, I don't see the harm in you having the help of one or two of your friends."

"How about three?"

"Fine." Her tone suggested it was far from it, but since she wouldn't be there in person, it didn't matter as much. "I will make the arrangements for you to have access with three guests. Be at the west entrance by eight thirty sharp. Any earlier or later, and you will not be let in." She hung up before I could ask her who we were meeting if it wasn't her.

With several hours between now and then, I could go check on the stalls at our big barn of shops even though it wasn't my day to run them. Or I could go back to bed and attempt to get as much rest as possible so I could be at my best tonight.

"Watch out, Buddy," I called out to the family cat. "I'm coming to join you."

CHAPTER SEVENTEEN

The girls and I finished eating our shrimp burgers from Mel's Drive Thru in Crystal's car while parked at the coven building. I stole a few fries from Dani and stuffed them in my mouth before she could slap my hand. Stolen fries were the best.

"We've got one more minute if you trust the time on my dashboard," Crystal announced. "Maybe we should go ahead and be waiting at the door."

We piled out and tossed our trash in a nearby bin as we walked by. Dani wiped ketchup off the corner of my lip despite my thievery, like a good cousin should.

"Do we knock?" Cate asked, staring at the large wooden door.

I shrugged. "I'm going to follow Ebonee's instructions to the letter. She said be at the west door by eight thirty sharp. And here we are."

"Uh, Rue? This is the east door," Crystal pointed out.

"Holy Hexes!" I cried, hustling to make it to the other side of the building as fast as my legs could carry me.

Cate, a regular runner, passed by me and got to the portico first. I followed behind Crystal, and Dani and I arrived last, our chests heaving from the effort.

The door creaked open, and a sliver of light beamed out into the dark. "I've been told to expect a Ruby Mae Jewell."

Still panting, I raised my hand. "That's me."

The door opened wider and a voice invited us in. We heard a click from the wall, and the hallway lights flickered on. "If you'll follow me, I'll take you to the member library."

Crystal bumped her hip against mine. "Are we being escorted by a ghost?" Her eyes flitted to the translucent figure wearing a simple skirt and a blouse with a bow at the collar floating in front of us.

Dani and I both shrugged, used to a lot more spectral presence in our lives. "I'm sorry, I didn't catch your name," I said. "These are my friends Crystal and Cate, and that's my cousin Danielle."

Our footsteps reverberated through the empty building until we got to a set of double wooden doors with ornate carvings over it. Our guide paused at the entrance and waited for us to give her our full attention.

"What we have in here is for coven members only, of which I've been assured y'all fulfill the requisite by the current leader. When you pass through these doors, your intent will be judged. If you come here seeking anything other than knowledge to grow as a witch and benefit the good of the coven, then you will not be permitted to enter. I suggest you take a moment to calm yourselves before you enter." She passed through the wooden barriers, leaving us on the outside.

With a quiet click, the door unlatched and creaked open. Taking a deep breath, I volunteered to test out the system. "I'll go first." I concentrated on my purpose to learn more about spellbinding to help Gloria, and in the long run Azalea and Harrison.

As I walked past the threshold, a slight tingle pressed against me. Without pausing, I continued until I stood on the other side. "I'm fine, girls, just walk through with clear intent."

The ghost shushed me. "This is a library," she reminded me.

Once all of us were inside, we took the time to look around. Dark stained tables were situated in the middle of the floor with more comfortable wing chairs dotting the immediate landscape. A few cubicles provided more privacy for anyone who came to read through the numerous volumes resting on stacks and shelves surrounding us.

"That's a lot of books," Crystal exclaimed. "How are we going to find what we need in one night?"

The spectral guide closed the door and faced us with a grin on her ghostly face. "All you have to do is tell me what you're looking for and I'll know right where to point you. I'm sorry for all the mystery, but until new visitors to the library have been tested, I try not to waste time going through my usual explanations."

Her new demeanor eased my initial tension. "I guess we should introduce ourselves again."

She held up her hand. "No need. I remember Crystal, Cate, and your cousin Danielle. Which makes you Ruby Mae Jewell." The spirit touched her chest. "I'm Marcia Gandry, the former and I suppose ongoing librarian, and it will be my pleasure to help you find whatever you need."

"It's a pleasure to meet you, Ms. Gandry," I said, gesturing at the books surrounding us. "But how did our small regional coven create such a large collection of resources?"

The ghost vanished and reappeared by the desk in the middle of the expansive space. "You can read all about the history of the library in these pamphlets when you come back with more leisure time on your hands. Simply put, the leader of the coven in the fifties, Professor Calvin Rockwell, liked to accumulate books and resources. He thought the strength of a coven lay in the knowledge they contained. When he passed, he bequeathed his entire collection, which provided the building blocks of what you see here."

Maybe later I would return to dig through any sources that could help me understand my fire talents better since I'd missed out on learning from my missing mother. "We need your best books about spellbinding."

Marcia shimmered out of sight and emerged again at my elbow. "Since you passed the test to come in, I can assume you are trying to expand your knowledge of the outlawed magic."

"It's illegal to make someone spellbound?" Dani asked. "What's the punishment for the crime?"

The librarian wavered in the air with a happy countenance. "These are things you can learn if you look in the right place. Along with legal consequences, I would advise you to also study the history behind how it came to be banned in civilized magical society, and then focus on some case studies."

She escorted each of us to the different bookcases, and the stacks of books piled higher than our heads when we sat down to study. "How will we ever get through all of these? We don't have months to read them all," Cate complained. "My plants at home will wither without me."

"How much time do you have, ladies?" Marcia asked. "A serious subject like this deserves your utmost attention for as long as possible if you're to gain a full understanding."

I glanced at the clock on the wall. "Well, I didn't intend to stay the entire night, but we kinda need to know everything as soon as possible."

"I'm afraid I was only authorized to let you stay until midnight," the librarian explained with sadness. "Perhaps you can make another entreaty to the coven leader to come back another time as well."

The longer we waited, the more chance the guilty party might get away. For all we knew, he or she could have been long gone, leaving Gloria behind to take the fall.

Out of desperation, I disobeyed Ebonee's order to keep things private, hoping that the amiable ghost knew how to stay silent. "This is more important than you can imagine, and we're running out of time. We have a friend we want to help who we think has been spellbound. Ms. Johnson is with this friend right now at the nearest warden facility."

The librarian's corporeal being wavered with shock. "It has been a long time since I've heard of any witch attempting powerful magic like that. Based on the whispers and rumors circulating throughout the membership, I can only guess who the players are that are involved." She unbuttoned her spectral sleeves and rolled them up. "I have a way for you to get to the information faster, but I'd prefer if you don't tell others about this method."

We followed her beckoning finger to the front desk. She unlocked the bottom drawer and pulled it out. Reciting a magical password, the bottom of the drawer dropped open, and a bundle of fabric fell onto the floor. With permission, Dani picked it up and unwrapped the contents. Two magnifying glasses rested in the middle of the cloth.

"Those are bespelled to find exactly what it is you

want to know. Whichever two are going to use them, you hold them over the open book and tell it what you need to know. It will flip through to the specific pages," Marcia instructed.

Crystal volunteered to use one of the magnifying glasses as did Dani, leaving Cate and I to be the readers. We got to work and narrowed down the most helpful books, putting back the ones with either brief mentions of spellbinding or repeated information from better sources.

Dani got caught up reading one of the passages her magnifying glass flipped to. "It says here that spellbinding was generally thought to only be used by the most powerful or the highest in rank witches throughout history. But those are only the cases that made it into written record. There were probably thousands of people who attempted to bend someone's will that never got noticed."

"Or the caster or victim died because of it," Cate whispered. "I haven't found any examples where the person who was spellbound survived."

The gravity of our quest stopped all of us, the silence of the empty building weighing down on our shoulders. "Oh, Gloria," I uttered, pinching the bridge of my nose. "Even if we're able to figure out how it all happened, they still might not be able to do anything for her?"

The librarian hovered closer to us. "I'm sorry, I know I shouldn't be eavesdropping. It's terrible etiquette for one of my profession, but I think I may have misled your search by giving you more history. It's my desire for people to learn as much from the past to help them inform and change the future. But I didn't mean for you to lose hope for your friend. If one of you will follow me, I can get you better books."

Crystal returned with three more tomes to search through. Her shoulders slumped with relief. "Oh, good. Here's a written case from the eighties where the spellbound victim didn't die and was even instrumental in finding the culprit."

Dani took one of the other books and gave her magnifying glass the same search parameters. "Here's another one. And right here, it says that with more modern ways to record or communicate with more people, the details of spellbinding were shared for healers to use to help those afflicted. It was also in the twentieth century when some of the strictest laws were created to punish those who were caught."

I raised my hand to garner Marcia's attention. "These are all good references, but is there something that could summarize it all? Like a step-by-step instructional of how one would even attempt a spellbinding? Or what it takes to make it work?"

"We don't need an encyclopedic explanation. We've learned a lot already." Cate pointed at a book she'd laid to her right side. "Usually, the spellcaster had to be near their victim. Only a handful of records exist of a witch who spellbound someone from a great distance, and they were noted as being someone of great importance or strength in magic."

I considered the books I'd read through. "And, I don't know if you noticed, but there seem to be some common themes of why people were spell-bound. Love, money, or power were at the top." That realization would narrow down the list of possibilities by a mile. "I'll need to talk more with Harrison to see if he can produce a list of suspects now that he's home."

"Azalea will be thrilled," Crystal snarked. "She's been a little possessive of his time. When I brought by a cute coffee mug I thought would make him laugh with a cartoon of an older woman wearing a bikini and laying by the ocean that said *Beach, Please*, she kicked me out. I think being cooped up with him is getting to her a little."

I rubbed my stiff neck and stood up to stretch. "What time is it?"

"Almost midnight. We'll be kicked out of here soon." Cate followed my lead, complaining about the soreness of her behind.

Panicked, I thumbed through the book in front of me. "We've got some plausible reasons we can work with. But what about how the spell is cast in the first place?"

"I said the caster would have to be close to the victim," Cate repeated. "But I read at least two accounts where the initiating spell was put into an object the victim kept on them. Like in one of the stories, it was a wedding ring."

"Ew, someone spellbound their spouse?" Dani asked. "That's all kinds of horrible."

Giving it too much consideration with our time winding down, I wouldn't have put it past Dad to try and spellbind my mother to get her to stay if he weren't such an honest man. "Love or passion can be a powerful catalyst."

Marcia materialized. "I'm sorry, ladies, but I must ask you to take your last minutes to return the books to their rightful places."

I pleaded with her, hugging one of the books to my chest. "Can we have just a few more moments? I think we were really onto something based on your superb recommendations."

The ghost clasped her hands in front of her and bowed her head with more apologies. "That will not be possible. If you can receive authorization again, I'm sure you can come back, and I'll be happy to assist you."

Dani wrapped the magnifying glasses in the fabric and returned to the desk. The librarian accompanied her to secure the instruments of examination to their hiding place.

It wasn't Marcia's fault we hadn't completed our task in one night. And maybe Ebonee would allow me to come back, even if that meant a further delay in saving Gloria. But as we finished cleaning up, I felt like I'd failed our friend.

On our way out the door, the librarian stopped me. "From what I heard, you gained much more knowledge than you possessed when you entered. Focus on that positive note rather than mourning what you have yet to learn. Also, please give my kind regards to your great-grandmother."

A slight smile replaced my grim scowl. "You know Granny Jo?"

"I suspect most everybody in this area has a relative who knew her." The ghost grinned. "Her reputation of being one of the strongest healers reached far and wide, and she helped me when I was really young. I think she might have been one of the few non-members ever given access to the library before or since."

"I'll pass along your salutations," I promised. "Thanks for all your help tonight. Including the shortcut magnifying glasses." I placed my finger to my lips to reiterate my silent promise to her.

We trudged to the other side of the building and got in Crystal's car, exhausted and worn out. Driving back, we maintained a tense silence, caught up in what we'd read and trying to figure out how to move forward. An idea planted itself in my head, and I let it germinate until we got to Cate's house to drop her off.

Following the librarian's advice, I focused on what we had learned. Based on that knowledge, I asked my friends for a favor. "I think we can work with what we've got right now. But I'm gonna need your help tomorrow evening."

Crystal rubbed her hand down her face. "Odie won't like me gone two nights in a row."

I squeezed her arm. "I think we can accomplish what I need without you."

"And what's that?" Dani asked, rubbing her hands together.

I pointed at my cousin and Cate. "You two are going to get Azalea out of the house. I need some time alone with Harrison."

CHAPTER EIGHTEEN

I waited around the corner from Harrison and Azalea's place, watching the front door to observe when Azalea left the premises. Dani's brother's big F-150 sat in the driveway. Deacon would cuss us both out for using it, but what that pig didn't know wouldn't hurt him.

Azalea had flat out refused to leave her recovering husband's side when my cousin first called. After filling Wesley in on our plan and assuring him that everything we were doing was to narrow down the search for the person who hurt his sister, he assisted us by pushing his best friend to encourage his wife to get out of the house, even for a short amount of time.

The lights on the truck flashed, and I hunkered

down in Gloria's car that I'd yet to take back to her garage. Dani exited the house first and opened the driver's side door. Cate appeared, dragging Azalea by the arm. They stopped at least a couple of times in the few feet between the front door and the vehicle.

"Come on," I coached from inside the car, not caring if they could actually hear me. "Get her in the truck. Tie her up and throw her in the back of the bed if you have to."

Cate opened the passenger door and boosted Azalea into the seat, her hands pushing the rear of the resistant bride. She shut the door and shot an exasperated look in my direction, crawling into the smaller backseat. I counted down the seconds before they passed by me.

My spell phone pinged. *Left the front door unlocked - C"*

I got out of my friend's borrowed car and snuck across the street as if on a clandestine mission. No nosy neighbors watched me through their windows, and I approached the front door, knocking once and entering without waiting for an invitation.

"Did you get cold feet, honey bear?" Harrison called out from around the corner. "I told those girls you wouldn't make it ten minutes."

With quiet steps, I entered the living room. "My feet are plenty toasty, Boo Boo."

He paused the movie on the television and moved the recliner into a more upright position. "What are you doing here? And how did you get in?"

"These are unimportant questions." I grabbed a chair from their dining table and dragged it over to sit next to him. "How ya feeling? Need to go to the bathroom or anything?"

"When did you become my charge nurse?" Harrison set his bowl of popcorn on the side table. "What's this all about, Rue? Is this why the other girls forced my wife to go out?" He placed his hands on the arms of the chair and grunted while trying to stand up.

I held onto him. "Don't. I'll explain everything, but I knew this would be better if your brand-new wife didn't hear me making requests of you like giving me the list of all the girls who could possibly want to kill you."

My bluntness earned his steely silence. He swallowed hard and relaxed back into the recliner. "Yeah, I don't think I'd like you saying something like that around Azalea. And honestly, I don't mind that she's gone. She needs a break from taking care of me."

Before I pumped him for information, I offered

to get him anything he needed to stay comfortable. It took me a second to realize my stalling tactics. What I had to ask would rank pretty high on the awkward scale. I gave him the rundown of what had happened so far, surprised Wesley hadn't filled him in about Gloria.

"I had no idea. Well, I had a little after you left, but neither of us could believe that she would hurt me." Harrison squirmed in discomfort. "But you think she wasn't in her right mind?"

"The term is spellbound, and from what I've researched, the witch who did this to both Gloria and you had to be pretty motivated for it to even work." I leaned on the arm of his chair. "Would you believe that we think whoever did this messed up pretty bad? Which is why I think it's possible to catch them, but I need your help."

He stared off in front of him, digesting everything he was told. "I get why you wanted my wife out of the house. She'd have a nuclear meltdown, she's been so worried about Gloria. If she wasn't obsessing about making sure I'm okay every second of every day, she would have already been on the case."

"I know," I admitted. "It's for Gloria but also for you as a couple. The sooner we can bring this to an end, the quicker you can get on with your lives. And you're at the center of all of it."

Harrison pointed at a desk on the wall opposite us. "There's a pad of paper and a pen or pencil in there. Let's get started. Who knows how long Azalea will make it before she bugs her friends to bring her back."

My former colleague's past love life would be a minefield. I stuck with the other common motivators we'd surmised from our time at the coven library. "Was there anyone you had a major quarrel with? Anyone you can think of who has threatened you or wished harm would come to you?" I steadied the pen over the paper, ready to take as many notes as needed.

"No, I can't think of anyone. I mean, you know how it is working at a bar. You get the occasional jerk who gets mad when you cut their drinks off. But I don't take what they say seriously," he said, scratching his head. "Me and Jay had a pretty good argument one night when his credit card wouldn't work."

The name sounded familiar, but I couldn't quite place it. "Do you mean Jay Fowler? Or that guy Jason who told everyone to call him Jay?"

"Fowler," Harrison confirmed. "He accused me of

using the card to steal money from him, but it turned out he and his wife were going through a divorce and she'd cut off that particular card that day."

I wrote down the incident. "When was this?"

He counted on his fingers while he thought. "A good six months ago. I mean, the guy was in nine kinds of emotional pain. He took an unsuccessful swing at me, but he's been back since then and we're all good."

Tapping the pen against the paper, I considered crossing off the name. Wanting more possibilities to look into, I left it at the top of the page. "Now that you're manager at the Tiki, have you had any problems with the other employees? Anyone you had to fire that might have wanted to get back at you?"

"We had one kid who worked for us last summer who was absolute crap at his job. He stole tips from others and did as little as possible while pulling in a paycheck." Harrison rubbed his chin. "But you know Roscoe. You practically have to kill someone before he lets you go."

"Nice choice of words," I smirked.

He wiggled his finger at me. "That wasn't breaking my promise. I wasn't saying it about me. You can't take the comic away."

I smacked him with the tip of the pen as a punishment. "Roscoe's good people. He gave all of us second, third, and fourth chances. And when we disappointed him, we felt it to our core. But when we earned his respect, we worked hard to be better."

"In my case, it was more like fifth, sixth, and seventh chances." Harrison wiped his brow with his hand. "And thank goodness. I wouldn't have moved up in the business without his encouragement."

Roscoe's passion for "his kids" was legendary. It's what kept some of us there working the tourist crowds for years. But out of all of us, he held Harrison to a higher standard. The boss had been hard on him for years, but it had all paid off.

"Why didn't Roscoe come to the wedding?" It hadn't occurred to me that my former boss hadn't been there.

"I told him not to." Harrison adjusted in his seat. "The man gets a little too emotional, and I think he didn't want to be seen as trying to stand in for my lack of family. He took me and Azalea out for a very nice dinner at Spinner's to celebrate prior to the wedding. That was enough for us."

"Aww." I couldn't contain my adoration for my former boss. I'd have to do something nice for him, even though he wouldn't know why. "Any money issues going on with you? Have you won some big lottery that someone would want to kill you over?"

Harrison glowered at me. "By that time, I was married. Anything that was mine would go to Azalea. And if we follow that logic, then she was the one who did it."

"Well…" It hadn't occurred to me to consider his new wife.

"Don't even go there. I mean it," he threatened. "If you had seen her ever since I've gotten home, you would know she wouldn't be capable of causing me harm like that. She'd do something to herself first, and you know that's true."

I did, and I regretted even spending one thought on the possibility. "Sorry," I uttered. "But the field of suspects is pretty thin." I showed him the pad with Jay's name on it.

"Then let's get down to the subject you first brought up. My past with girls." He fidgeted in the chair, his cheeks a brighter pink from embarrassment. "Off the top of my head, I'd put Cassidy Larkin at the top. But she was pretty cool with all the flowers she did for the wedding, so I don't know."

"We already checked her out before, and she and Gloria actually might be able to mend their friendship." I withheld the obvious fact that we had to save Gloria first.

Harrison glanced down at the notepad. "There's a pretty long list of girls I went out with. I'm not exactly proud of that side of my past. It might take you an entire year to find them all."

Wrinkling my nose, I tapped him on the arm again with the pen. "First, eww. Second, you were a pretty big player back in the day. Third, let's try to list those you went out with more than once. Or any that you can remember who might have tried to push you into a relationship."

He gave me three names of solid leads, but tortured me with the numerous names of girls who were one-night strangers and others that I knew and had no idea he'd been with.

"Well, that was a terrifying trip down Disgusting Lane." I vetoed the last name because I already knew she no longer lived in the area in more than five years. "Can you think of anyone who maybe obsessed over you? Maybe you got a lot of crank calls or hang ups? Somebody left you gifts or notes?"

"Notes!" Harrison exclaimed. "Yes, I would get these odd notes from time to time. I didn't think anything of them because they wouldn't say anything more than wishing me a good day or complimenting what I wore."

"That's pretty creepy. Were you so full of yourself that you didn't recognize a stalker when you had one?" My heart beat fast at the hint of a real lead. "It would be too much to ask if you happen to have any of those notes still, right?"

He tilted his head and scoffed. "Do you honestly believe that I would keep a bundle of those hidden somewhere in this house for Azalea to find one day? I know I haven't always been the brightest bulb, but surely you can't believe I'm that stupid."

I held up my hands in surrender. "That's not why I asked. If you did still have a note, then we'd have the handwriting of the person who might have spellbound Gloria."

"Oh. That makes sense." He bit his thumbnail. "I started getting them right after high school. No pattern to when they'd show up or where. They were always written in the neatest swirling cursive script, so I knew they had to be from a girl."

"And because you liked female attention, you never thought about the person who actually gave them to you. That they might not be completely healthy, giving notes to you all those years."

Harrison threw his hands in the air. "Fine. I've

been a totally self-obsessed slimeball. But that's why I would never do anything to jeopardize what I have with Azalea."

Another chime rang from my purse and I checked the message. "Crap. Cate and Dani weren't able to keep your wife out for very long. She's on her way back, and I think you'd agree, it's better not to worry her with any of this."

Tearing off the paper from the pad, I replaced the notebook and pen back on the desk where I'd found them and did the same with the chair.

"I wish I'd been more help, Rue. Because whoever it is that did this to both me and Gloria, they deserve to pay." Harrison's eyes burned with the need for revenge.

"Don't worry. Based on what I've read, if we can catch this person, according to witch law, they'll be more than punished for their crime against the two of you." I waved at him and hurried out the front door and across the street.

If the magical law didn't catch up to whomever it was, then the cost for abusing magic would eventually get them. But that didn't guarantee Gloria's safety or recovery from the damage already perpetrated against her.

My spell phone lit up on the darkened street, and

I read Cate's message that they were almost here. Opening up the door to Gloria's car, I slunk inside and ducked down as the light from my cousin's truck blazed a path to the newlywed's house.

I waited for what felt like hours for Dani to pull out of the driveway. She flashed her lights as they drove by, and I typed out that I would meet them at my place.

Turning the engine on, I drove around the corner before I flipped on the lights. A piece of paper fluttered underneath the driver's side windshield wiper. I slowed down and pulled off to the side of the street so I could retrieve it. Once I had it in my hand, my heart almost exploded with excitement. I turned on the interior light and examined it carefully.

In perfect swirling cursive, I read the message written especially for me. *"Stay away from Harrison. He's mine."*

CHAPTER NINETEEN

Uncle Jo jumped off the back of Ol' Bessie with a grunt. "I'm getting too old for this job," he complained, pulling the last box off the truck bed. "And if that rooster comes at me again, he's gonna find himself fried and eaten."

"You'll lose out on all those eggs the hens have been laying," I said, checking my surroundings to make sure that sneaky little fowl was nowhere near me.

"We can get another one," my uncle insisted. "It was funny at first to have a chicken guarding the barn from unwanted visitors or bragging we had a guard rooster. Now, it's just ticking me off." He pulled up his jeans to show me his ankles. "He's pecked an entire chunk out of me."

"Then you need to convince your son to hang around more. Deacon's the only being in this world Rex likes." For whatever reason, that freak of nature bird adored my pig of a cousin.

Uncle Jo hauled the box into the barn. "If it were one of the hens, I might understand why." He peeled open the flaps and dug inside. "Heads up, here comes your daddy."

My father waved a brown envelope at me then used it to shoo away Rex, who clucked a warning prior to a possible attack.

I cupped my hands around my mouth. "You could always hex his feathers right off his hide. That might take his orneriness down a notch."

"Or prepare him to be fried up in a skillet," Dad countered.

Uncle Jo snorted and stacked a bunch of leather-bound books on the workbench. "I just said almost the same thing."

"It's like you two are brothers. Weird," I teased, giving my father a quick kiss on the cheek. "What's in the envelope?"

My father held it up to his head. "Wait, wait, let me see. I'm such a strong psychic that I can almost… Nope. It's gone," he joked. "It's addressed to you anyway, butter bean."

I tore off the top seam of the package and pulled out a letter handwritten in messy print. "It's from Mac, the keyboardist of Tailgate Down." My eyes skimmed the note so fast, I thought I'd misunderstood it. Forcing myself to slow down, I read it again with greater care.

RM -

We were prepping for another gig in town and Levi found these in one of our cases. Pretty sure they're the request slips from the reception since we had to pack up so quickly. Was going to throw them away but sent them to you because I thought you could decide if they're useful or not. Keep us posted, and we hope to see you sooner rather than later. - Mac

Breathless, I tossed the letter on the table. My shaking hands dropped the envelope, and I swore as a slip of paper fell out onto the ground. A slight breeze caught the thin vellum and blew it out of the barn. "Grab that!" I ordered, chasing after it and not caring if Rex tried to draw blood from my ankles.

Buddy dashed out of nowhere and stood between me and the feisty rooster. His back arched and his hair stood on end. He hissed at Rex through his tiny mustached mouth and bat his paw in the air to show he meant business.

"Good boy, Buddy. You earned at least two cans of tuna for saving me," I cooed at him, backing away into safety. The cat zipped inside with me at the last second, and I shut the door behind us.

"Why did you risk your life for a scrap of paper?" Uncle Jo asked.

I moved the stack of books out of the way and dumped the rest of the contents from the envelope onto the rickety table. "Because these are the requests from the night of the wedding reception. It may be absolutely nothing, but at least it's one more concrete thing to check."

The threatening note I'd found under the windshield wiper had felt like a step forward. But unless I wanted to compare it to the handwriting of every single witch up and down the entire Crystal Coast, it taunted me with the inability to put it to good use to find whoever wrote it. The only positive thing that came out of knowing Harrison's stalker had been there was reporting it to Ebonee, who passed it on to the lieutenant. I hoped our friends hadn't noticed the uptick in patrol cars passing by their house.

Wishing I had Mac's timeline with me, I sorted through the requests, recognizing the majority of them. The playlist in my head switched with each paper I read as if I were changing the dial on the radio in the truck.

I got through the entire pile and stuffed them back in the envelope. "Dang blast it, there's nothing here worth saving. Might as well torch these." A curl of smoke billowed out of the corner of the envelope I gripped between my fingers until a tiny flame smoldered to life.

"Wait, don't burn our entire barn down with your disappointment," Uncle Jo warned, backing away from me. "And you missed one right at your feet."

The ember of my tantrum-induced flame burned out, and I bent down to retrieve the last request. Unfolding the wrinkled piece, I screeched at its simple content. Written in the same cursive script as the warning I'd gotten after seeing Harrison was the title of that one song that didn't fit with any of the others.

Dropping the package on the ground, I pumped a fist in the air. "Yes!" I shouted. The precious paper almost slipped my grip in my excitement, and I stopped celebrating to keep from losing it.

Dad peeked over my shoulder. *Shoulda Known Better*. That's a country song, right? But why are you acting like you just found a winning lottery ticket?"

I jumped up and down with giggling squeals. "Because this is a prize. It's absolute proof that the person I'm pretty sure spellbound Gloria and tried to hurt or even kill Harrison was there that night." Holding out the paper for my father and uncle to read, I pointed at the script. "See that cursive? It's a complete match for the note left on Gloria's car."

"I might be able to see it if you'd quit your bouncin'," my uncle ribbed me with a little extra twang in his Southern accent. His phone rang, and he switched to his professional voice. "Hello, you've reached Josephus Jewell. How may I help you?" After a few nods and *uh-huh's*, he pointed his finger at me. "Yes, I can make sure Ruby Mae is with us. I think we can be there within the next hour if that works for you. You, too," he finished and hung up.

"Who was that?" Dad asked, picking up the envelope I'd dropped.

"And why are you volunteering me when I clearly need to contact Ebonee to share my news and maybe take this over to the lieutenant?" I complained, fondling the strip of paper in my hand.

"That was Robin Westwood. She wants us to come over to her shop. And she wants you there specifically." Uncle Jo hustled to organize the rest of the contents of the box, nudging me out of his way with his girth.

The request threw me off. "That's strange. She told me she was thinking about closing the shop in the next year or so. This is more than a little unexpected. But I guess it doesn't matter when we give her an estimate."

"She doesn't want an evaluation of her property. The lady said she wanted us to come and claim what we thought we could resell for her at a good price." My uncle shrugged. "A job's a job."

Not that long ago, I'd sat on her couch while she admitted she was ready. But I figured if she had wanted to move this fast, she would have said so then.

"What's got you riled up, butter bean? You've got that determined glint in your eyes," my father stated.

"You're definitely going with us, right, Dad? I want to make sure she's making the right decision before we go taking anything. And that we can do right by her in the long run." I'd have to have them drive by my house first so I could stash the precious strip of paper somewhere safe before we left.

"I can if that will make you happy," my father agreed. "And we'd never take advantage if you think she's not in her right mind. You go with your gut, and we'll follow your lead."

Nothing about Ms. Robin's decision sat well with me, and despite the nature of our business, I refused to be a vulture picking over the bones of her business.

CHAPTER TWENTY

We arrived at the dress shop forty-five minutes later. Dad and I got out while Uncle Jo drove around the block to find a better parking place for the large work truck. A handwritten sign on the glass door read "Closed." I tried the handle of the door. Locked.

Shielding my eyes, I peered inside, curious and worried about what I'd find. All of the dresses hung on the same racks and rows as before. There was no indication why Ms. Robin would be closing her business other than the taped-up sign and the lack of lights on inside.

I wrapped my knuckle against the glass and stood back, waiting. Movement caught my eye, and I spotted Ms. Robin walking over to let us in. She reached up on her tiptoes to flip the top lock and bent over to unhitch the bottom one. With a light click, she turned the final one by the door handle and gestured for us to come in.

"I'm sorry to bother you or pull you from another job," she apologized, allowing us to walk past her.

My father introduced himself and then my uncle when he sauntered in. The normalcy of the moment ruffled my feathers, and I skipped right past the pleasantries. "I thought you had a plan, Ms. Robin."

"Plans change," she replied, shuffling away with her shoulders stooped as if she carried the weight of the world on them. "After what happened at Azalea's wedding and Tara losing her mind, I'd rather close now than be disappointed or upset by anything else. I've already referred clients who wanted dresses in the near future, and I have one that I'll finish up today so you can take my sewing machine with you."

I gasped at her final edict. When she'd spoken about the machine before, it was like it had become an extended part of her. Now, she wanted us to amputate it from her life.

"Who's Tara?" Dad whispered to me.

"Her assistant," I explained, wanting to get back to the problem at hand.

Ms. Robin jolted when she heard my reply. "Not anymore. Tara quit on me in a fit of what I can only describe as lunacy. She's always been a bit more emotional, but she had some decent skills. I thought she wanted to pursue a career in fashion, but nobody will work with her after this. I'll make sure of it."

A tense silence followed her passionate tirade. My uncle took the opportunity to walk around the showroom, sizing up the inventory. Dad ran a finger down the back of my hand in encouragement and joined his brother to give me space.

"I thought you liked Tara. What happened to change your mind?" I pushed in a quieter voice.

"This." The woman turned her head so I could see the left side of her face. A dark bruise marred her cheek. "One second, I was comforting her because she fell apart after she told me she was quitting. And then she snapped at me, demanding that I give her my sewing machine because I'd promised to help her step up in her career. I thought she was kidding, so I laughed. I never saw her fist coming or I might have taken the first shot."

"Ms. Robin!" I exclaimed.

"I'm from New York. I know how to handle myself," she sniffed, her fingertips brushing her swollen cheek. "I told her I would report her to the police for assault and battery, and that scared Tara enough to realize what she'd done. She fell to her knees and begged me not to do it. Said that everything in her life was going wrong, and that she didn't know how to fix it. At that point, I figured her problems were her own, and I asked her to leave."

My dad sidled up to listen in, and I continued. "Did she go, or did you have her arrested?"

"She left." Ms. Robin dropped her head, squeezing her eyes shut. "I thought I'd feel better after it happened, but I just can't shake the feeling that I should have found a way to get through to her. To try and help."

I stroked her arm in sympathy. "Some people will say they want help but can't accept it."

The designer considered my words, looked up at the ceiling, and groaned. "I tried calling her," she admitted. "But she's not picking up anymore. As far as I know, she's gone."

Uncle Jo joined us and coughed a couple of times. "Excuse me, ma'am, but I'm a little parched. I don't suppose you have any libations?"

Abhorred at her lack of manners, Ms. Robin rushed off to fetch us all some water bottles. I turned to my uncle to question the lie. "Okay, what was that all about?"

He placed his hands in his pockets and rocked back on his heels. "This is a rare occasion where I have to admit I might be wrong. She definitely went through something recently, and it's possible she's going to regret any decision she makes while under duress."

"That bruise looks bad, but I'll bet it looks worse in the light," Dad grumbled. "Did she have it checked out?"

"It's just a little swollen, Mr. Jewell," the designer replied with our drinks in her hands. "A bag of frozen peas and a stiff cocktail was the only treatment I needed. And I know you think I might be crazy to make such an impetuous decision to close shop, but I promise you, the only thing the whole incident did was change the when of it all."

"Are you sure?" I double-checked. "We can always take a look at what you have now and come back later."

She shook her head. "You might as well be making your offer to a brick wall. When I make up my mind, that's it. Kinda like how I gave up New York and came down here in the first place. I up and left without warning to claim my Buster and move here. Best decision I ever made. My gut tells me this one will be, too."

I opened my mouth again, but my father tapped my arm to stop me. "Then can you walk us around and give us an idea of your expectations? I hate to admit it, but I don't think selling your creations in our barn would be the smartest choice."

"I'll be responsible for what I want to do with my creations. Maybe have a blowout sale so local brides can find their dresses at a discount. Especially those who, as I heard it, caught a wedding bouquet recently." She beamed at me, a little of her old self seeping back in.

"It was a total set up," I complained when my father and uncle joined her in teasing me about becoming a bride.

"Follow me to see the rest of my property. It used to be a separate business back in the day, but I bought it and turned it into storage and my workspace." She pointed out a few items like naked mannequins and some empty clothes racks we could haul away today.

For such a small operation, Ms. Robin possessed a lot of stuff. Lucky for us, she liked to be organized, making it easy for us to start a list of potential items. She got caught up in explaining the different kinds of fabric and how each of them would drape differently off a body.

"How long does it take you to make a single dress like Azalea's or Gloria's?" I asked, touching the end of some soft satin fabric.

Ms. Robin's eyes twinkled. "I loved working on Azalea's dress. That lovely shade of blush went perfectly with her skin tone. I shouldn't admit this, but I liked helping her rebel a little against her mother after some of the stories that poor girl told me. But it took me the better part of seven months."

I hated the thought that Azalea's dress was folded up somewhere catalogued as a piece of evidence when the new bride wasn't even the one who did anything.

"What about the bridesmaids' dresses? How long did Gloria's take?"

"That style isn't custom since we used an existing pattern. Pieces like hers require a choice in color and some measurements to be put together," the designer explained. "Tara worked on those dresses. Which is another reason I'm closing down. With little time to train a new assistant, I don't have anyone else to help, and I'm a little too old to try and do everything myself."

My heart pounded in my ears. "I'm sorry, but did you say Tara made Gloria's dress?"

Ms. Robin caught the change in my voice. "Did

she do something wrong to it? I'd hate to think that her emotions got in the way of her work."

A wave of dizziness hit me as I made an important connection. I reached out to steady myself against a workstation. "No, Gloria's dress seemed fine."

The designer blew out a breath of relief. "Good. I worried a little when I caught Tara working on it at the last second. Somehow, I'd left the door unlocked to my private work area, and she was using my sewing machine, claiming the one she typically used wasn't working and she needed to fix the hem."

Her words barely registered with me as her former assistant's name echoed in my head. My stomach clenched and alarm bells went off. I followed behind Ms. Robin in a bit of a daze, listening to her ramble on about her work that she loved.

She pulled out a key and unlocked the door to a private room. She stood in front of a custom table made to fit around an antique cabinet with an old but beloved sewing machine on it. The woman ran a hand over its black surface with gold filigree embellishments and hand painted floral decorations.

"She's another example of a quick decision that turned out to be one of the best. I found her at the

Grand Bazaar flea market in Manhattan and paid extra to have them take her back to my tiny apartment I was working out of at the time." Her passion for the piece poured out of her, and I did my best to admire it.

"I said this before, but you can always take her with you," I suggested, reaching out to trace a swirl of gold paint. The second my fingertips touched the machine, a zing of energy bolted up my arm and the tiny hairs on it stood at alarmed attention.

Ms. Robin missed my reaction and sat down at the table. "It's time for her to grace someone else with her magic. All I need is to finish sewing up this hem, and I'll be done with her."

With the machine in use, I couldn't examine it as closely I needed to, now that everything had changed. She was right about one thing, even though she didn't know the full meaning of her words. The sewing machine definitely possessed magic. I searched for Dad and Uncle Jo to get their second opinions but could only hear their muffled voices coming from the other side of the storage space.

I paced behind Ms. Robin while she tucked a white strip of something at the bottom of her last dress and folded the navy-blue fabric over it, finishing the hem with slow stitches. Leaning over her shoulder, I tried for a better look. "What's that you're sewing in?"

She dismissed me with a chuckle. "Oh, it's a silly tradition. I like to write personal messages of good luck and well wishes and place them where they won't be noticed by the person wearing it. It's like giving them a piece of me that will make the time that they wear my creation a little more special."

"You do this with every dress?" I clarified, testing out a theory forming in my head.

Ms. Robin nodded and kept working. The table vibrated under the needle flying over the fabric. "Mm-hmm. Pretty much. Even sewed one into yours," she winked at me. "I just wished for you to live boldly and claim what was yours."

I recalled the feeling that washed over me when I put on the dress before going to the wedding. I'd never felt so confident or so beautiful, especially when Luke appreciated how I looked. Maybe a part of my emotions had been affected by Ms. Robin's hidden message she'd sewn in using a machine that hummed with power.

"There. Finished." She trimmed the thread and stood, holding up the final product. "I'll hold onto this for the client. But I guess this is it."

My father poked his head in and admired the

dress. "That's real pretty. Whoever it's for will look beautiful in it."

"Thank you, Mr. Jewell," she beamed. "I'll put this in a garment bag and then take it up front to wait for pick up."

I grabbed Dad's hand and dragged him outside to another worktable with a bolt of fabric spread out on its surface. "We've got to get that sewing machine out of here right now," I whispered through clenched teeth.

"Why?" he asked. "It's going to take a while to negotiate what she wants to do with the items we think we can sell. What's the rush?"

Ms. Robin excused herself to go up to the storefront, and I escorted my father over to the sewing machine. "Here's why." I grasped his hand and held it right over the decorated surface.

He flinched away. "Whoa. That thing has some kick to it."

"She just used it." I tapped his arm multiple times with my finger. "And, I think she's unintentionally been enchanting her pieces. I just watched her sew what she calls good wishes into the hem of that dress."

My father listened while he bent down to examine the machine. "But she's not a witch, is she?"

"No, but this thing might have taken her good intentions and turned them into magic." I paced around to the other side of the table and leaned on it. "Also, I'm pretty sure I've figured it out."

Uncle Jo joined us. "Figured what out? I can hear you guys all the way on the other side of the room even though you think you're whispering.

"Look at this, Jo," Dad insisted. "We're going to need an exit strategy to get out of here quicker than you and I planned."

I slapped my hands on top of the work surface to get their attention. "You're not listening to me. Based on the sewing machine, the notes in the dresses, and Ms. Robin's reasons for closing, I think I've figured out who's at the center of everything."

WE'D MADE EXCUSES ABOUT NEEDING MORE TIME TO do the job right but insisted on taking the sewing machine and its cabinet back with us to do a thorough examination of its condition to set the right price. I didn't doubt that our strange behavior tipped Ms. Robin off to something not being quite right, but she hadn't put up a fight. We let her have a moment with the machine before we removed it, waiting until we got it out in the truck before covering it up with neutralizing fabric.

It sat in the middle of the living room at the big house with the three of us standing around while Granny Jo drifted around it. "It's got a fair amount of power if you know what you're looking for. You say she bought this at a flea market?" she asked me.

I told her about the hidden messages, waiting with impatience for her to confirm my biggest suspicions.

"Sounds to me like she was able to cast some harmless spells, even though she's mortal." My ghostly granny admired the condition of the object. "Combining her intent with the energy from the machine created the magic. Thank goodness she's a good person with a kind heart, as you said. In the wrong hands, a lot of damage could be done."

"Like spellbinding another person?" I blurted out, too exhilarated to hold in my idea. "Listen, if I stitch all of the small pieces together, I think I'm right when I accuse Tara of being the witch who spellbound Gloria."

Granny Jo hovered in place. "You've got pretty good instincts, Ruby Mae. But what proof do you have?"

I ticked off my list with my fingers. "She was

acting funny about Harrison. She was the one who created Gloria's dress, and Ms. Robin said she'd caught her re-stitching the hem of it right before the wedding. And why would Tara turn on the boss she clearly admired and attack her for not wanting to sell her the sewing machine?"

The room fell silent while they considered my theory. Dad tapped his finger to the corner of his mouth. "All good points, but it's still speculation. You're lacking concrete evidence."

"I agree," murmured my uncle. "Maybe you should get your coven leader involved and see if she thinks it's worth proposing the idea to that warden woman."

I pulled my spell phone out of my pocket but hesitated before pulling up Ebonee's contact number. Although I didn't know all of the coven rules, I would bet there would be consequences if I accused a fellow member of a crime and then was wrong. Plus, I didn't want to make a fool out of myself and go back to being out of favor with Ebonee again.

"Granny, what's the best way to spellbind someone? Just by being near the person?" I asked.

My great-grandmother stopped inspecting the sewing machine. "If the spellcaster is strong enough, maybe. But most of the stories I heard involved an object that the victim would have on his or her person. Like jewelry."

"Or a dress," I exclaimed, jumping when my phone rang in my hand. Annoyed at the interruption, I answered it. "Hey, Wesley."

"Hey, do you still have Glo's car at your place?" he asked without hesitation.

With everything going on, I hadn't made the effort to get her car back to her garage yet. "Yeah, sorry about that."

He blew out a breath. "No, I'm actually glad that you do. I'm at her place right now, waiting for the police. Someone broke in here and tore it apart. I think you have what they were looking for in her car."

Granny Jo hovered close by so she could listen in. I moved away from her spectral presence. "What would that be?"

"The dress she wore for the wedding. I guess she had it with her when she took off and showed up at your place." A siren sounded in the background. "Listen, I don't know why Glo wanted me to get it. But I thought you should know in case it was there with you. I gotta go."

Ignoring my family's curiosity, I darted out of the

house and ran as fast as possible toward my cottage. Rex attempted to chase me when I approached the barn, but I bolted past him, listening to his disappointed clucks disappear behind me.

Out of breath but energized with purpose, I made it my place in less time than it would have taken to have my dad drive me here. Bursting through the front door, I found the keys to Gloria's car and used them to unlock the trunk. A garment bag with Ms. Robin's logo on it lay inside.

I yanked it out and brought it into my living room. Unzipping the bag, I pulled out the dress, fanning it out over the couch. With careful fingers, I checked the bottom hem and felt a familiar buzz of energy.

"If they want proof, now I got it," I announced, rushing off to find some scissors.

CHAPTER TWENTY-ONE

I crouched down behind a car parked on the same side of the road at Ms. Robin's shop. There had to be at least a good handful of wardens watching the store and waiting to catch Tara in the trap I'd helped plan. Despite my begging, I'd been told to let the professionals handle things. But I wanted the satisfaction of that sweet moment when she realized I was the one who took her down.

Picking the mailbox as my next target, I scampered over to duck down again. My hand fingered the key in my pocket that Ms. Robin had given my father so that we'd have access to her storeroom whenever we needed it. I might be pushing my family's personal code a little bit, but the payoff would make the future scolding worthwhile.

I stood up, prepared to sneak to the trash can attached to a light pole, and jumped at the voice behind me. "I thought I told you not to get involved," Lieutenant Alwin reprimanded. She spoke into her radio. "Not the suspect. Repeat. Not the suspect. Hold your positions."

"I should be there for the moment she gets caught and you know it," I protested. "I think I've earned it."

Grabbing me by my arm, she escorted me across the street by an unmarked car, forcing me to crouch down with her. "I compliment you on your cleverness, Ms. Jewell. Especially figuring out that the lyrics to the country song triggered Gloria into action. Between that and the other handwriting samples you collected, you pretty much handed us everything we needed to take her down."

Pride swelled in my chest and my cheeks heated. "Thank you."

"You might even make a decent warden candidate if I thought you could follow orders," she joked.

"I've got a good job, thank you." A little pride from her compliment dampened my frustration. "After what we've surmised about the sewing machine and its part in all of this, I think what we do is pretty important."

The lieutenant regarded me for an extra beat. "You're probably right. But you need to go home right now before—"

"Are you seriously involving a civilian in your operation, Lieutenant Alwin?" A flashlight shone in our faces, and Deputy Sheriff Caine approached the two of us.

"Caine, I don't have time for your nonsense right now." The lieutenant spoke into her radio. "And turn off that light."

With a click of a button, he obeyed but continued to rant. "I told the Sheriff you were up to something. I'll be filing a full report on allowing someone outside of law enforcement in on an operation. Ms. Jewell is the last person you want involved."

I didn't get a word of defense out before the lieutenant tore into him. "You are not the ranking officer here, Deputy. I'm aware of your constant surveillance of me, the things you've been saying to our colleagues, and your basic hounding over this entire case. If you want to move up in the organization, do it off your own merits, not by trying to tear me down."

His mustache twitched, but he wisely remained silent.

The lieutenant continued. "Furthermore, this is a

sanctioned cooperative operation between multiple city enforcement. Your exclusion from it should be quite obvious."

The radio she carried crackled once. "Uh, Lieutenant. A car just pulled up to the backdoor of the building."

"Maintain your positions. We want her to go inside so there's less of a chance for her to get away," Lieutenant Alwin instructed. She pointed at the deputy. "Caine, I need you to leave."

"I have more right than her to be here, but I'm the one being ordered to go," he complained, pointing a finger at me. "One more thing to go on my report."

"We don't have time for this." Without warning, the lieutenant flourished her hand and cast a spell on Deputy Caine. He slumped down against the side of the car, unconscious.

I gawked at her, a little impressed at her actions and a whole lot afraid of what she might do to me. "Didn't you just break a considerable amount of rules?"

"There's precedence for this, although it's not encouraged to knock a fellow officer out. Especially a mortal one." She grunted with the effort to move him into a seated position. "It's better to try and put together teams of other wardens when it comes to magical enforcement. Now, we'll have to waste time, effort, and resources dealing with the added problem of adjusting memories."

"Remind me not to tick you off," I muttered, scooting back a few inches and considering whether or not witnessing Tara get caught was worth the risk.

The lights flicked on inside the store, and someone in plain clothes opened the front door. "We've got her, Lieutenant," the warden called out.

I pleaded with my eyes to be allowed to go with her but braced myself for the order to leave. She regarded me for a long moment, then hung her head and shook it. "I guess if I'm already pressing the limits of my warden duties, you might as well tag along. Like you said, your exceptional work kind of earned you the right to witness the conclusion."

The entire front of the store with all of the merchandise was untouched. A few wardens milled about outside of Ms. Robin's private room, waiting. A couple of them that I recognized from the coven dipped their heads in respect. Entering the smaller room, the lieutenant and I found Tara sitting on a stool next to the decoy sewing machine my family and I had scrounged up to trap her.

"What's she doing here?" the girl hissed, squirming in her seat.

Her hands were bound behind her. The soft glow of the lights in the room lit up her sallow features. In such a short time, her appearance had changed, and I'm not sure I would have recognized her if we'd passed each other on the street in broad daylight.

"You're looking phenomenal, Tara. What's wrong? Been losing a lot of sleep?" I taunted.

"I said you could accompany me, not torture her," the lieutenant warned. "Let me do all the talking."

Shutting up so I could stay, I still managed to rile the girl up with a wink.

"I saw you there. At Harrison's house," Tara continued, aiming her venom at me. "It didn't take long for him to cheat on his wife. She was never good enough for him. Neither are you."

"And you are?" I muttered under my breath, shrugging an apology when the lieutenant glared at me.

"Miss Langston, have you been advised of your rights that anything you say can be used against you?" she asked.

Tara ignored the question, still talking only to me. "I've been his guardian all these years. Yes, he's been with a lot of women, but he was always going to choose me in the long run. Until that girl got in the way. And I had to play nice whenever she would come in for dress fittings." She paused and struggled against her restraints, causing a ruckus with the wardens.

"It seems she's only responding to you," Lieutenant Alwin turned around and spoke low enough for me to hear. "Before she wises up and stops talking, I'd like for you to ask as many helpful questions as possible."

Given the green light, my heart raced with anticipation. Once Tara settled back down, I drilled her without mercy. "When did you first figure things out about the sewing machine?"

She stuck her nose in the air. "Not that long after I began working here."

I doubted the truth behind her bravado, but I waited for her to continue.

"At first, I thought no harm could be done with those stupid little notes Robin would sew into her dresses. In fact, I didn't report it to the coven because it was an idea I intended to continue when she gave me the machine to start my own business someday." She cast her eyes to the floor. "I'd been waiting so patiently and acting like I cared about my job."

"Had Ms. Robin really promised she would give it to you?" I pressed.

Tara's attention returned to me. "I would have convinced her in the long run. Good plans take time to execute."

A little pity fractured my fury at her. How long had she been pining for Harrison and making plans for a fantasy that could never come true? I'd bet good money he didn't even know who she was, and yet she'd been leaving him notes and building her delusion for far too long.

"I don't think you took your time when you made your plan to use Gloria," I said, wanting to get to the heart of it all.

An eerie smile slithered across her lips. "Yes and no. I'd spent ages at the coven library, trying to discover a way to make Harrison mine. I lied to that stupid ghost that I wanted to learn all about how thread and weaving have been used in magic throughout history."

"What, you thought you could find the recipe to some love potion that would make him forget Azalea and finally see you?" The depths of her insanity revealed itself piece by piece.

She ignored my taunt. "I didn't even think about the possibility of spellbinding someone until

Harrison brought Azalea her purse during one of her fittings. I tried talking to him, but he dismissed me with polite chit chat instead of really seeing me right there next to him."

"He hurt you. I get that." I attempted a little compassion to keep her speaking.

Tara slumped on the stool. "Nobody sees me. I'm always in the background. The assistant. The one people don't think to invite."

For a brief second, I considered how difficult it might be to go through life feeling dismissed. But nothing excused her hurting other people. "If you loved Harrison, why did you spellbind Gloria to hurt him?"

"Because I couldn't bring myself to do it," Tara replied, a fat tear rolling down her face. "I'd been so happy to hear all the trouble about her parents and how many fights it started between them. I hoped it would break them apart, but it just brought them closer."

It still made no sense to me why she would go after the person she wanted, but I was thankful she hadn't tried to harm Azalea.

"You wanted to stop your pain," the lieutenant interjected. "That's why the groom was your intended target. And Gloria was just the vehicle to carry out your wishes."

"I didn't care if she got hurt in the process," Tara spit out with a grimace of disgust. "I knew every single thing about the wedding. So, I stitched in the spell with the lyrics from that song using the sewing machine into Gloria's dress. All I had to do was make sure the band played it, and everything would be taken care of."

She'd written the lyrics of the song onto a white strip of fabric much like Ms. Robin did with her well wishes. When I'd torn apart Gloria's dress, I found the prophetic words chosen with alarming purpose written in cursive across the long strip.

> "You should have plunged a knife into
> my breast
> Carved my heart out of my chest
> For all the pain you made me feel
> I shoulda known better."

"Were you happy when Gloria didn't actually kill him? Or were you afraid you'd get caught?" I asked, no longer able to find even a shred of pity for her. "Or maybe both?"

The tears stopped falling fast enough that I

wondered whether they had been real or not. She sat up a little straighter. "I think I'm done talking."

The lieutenant instructed her team to take Tara to the nearest warden station for processing. She also asked two of the guys to collect Deputy Sheriff Caine and take him as well since he'd have to undergo some spell modifications.

I followed her into the front of the store where she stopped with her hands on her hips, gazing at all of the beautiful dresses. "It's a lot harder to get that happy ending than the fairy tales make it out to be."

"There definitely aren't any clear pathways nor any shortcuts," I added. "My family instilled in me that anything worth getting is worth the hard work and made so much sweeter by the journey."

Lieutenant Alwin escorted me out of the store, allowing other wardens to lock up behind us. "Sounds like good advice. Thanks for your assistance in there. I think we picked up more than enough."

"I appreciate the opportunity." I drew in a long breath and let it out. "I think it might have killed me not to confront her."

The lieutenant stuck out her hand. "I still say you'd make a fine warden, but I think you're exactly where you need to be. Good luck, Miss Jewell."

We parted ways, and I took a few private

moments to replay the conversation with Tara in my head. I might never understand all her reasons behind what she did. Trying to figure her out might drive me crazy, and I didn't need to waste another second on her.

Once in the truck, I knew I should make a few calls or gather my friends to give them the news. But I needed to blow off a little steam first and clear my head. Turning on the radio, I flipped channels until I found the right song. There was very little in this world that a little Dolly couldn't solve.

Aiming the truck in the direction of the beach, I let the music and the wind wash over me and sang my way back to my normal life and my home.

D ad tugged at the tie around his neck. "I don't understand why we needed to dress up fancy."

"If I have to wear a dress, you have to at least wear a nice jacket and tie," I countered, straightening the striped necktie back into place.

"Whoever it is that's showing up, they're going to have to take me as I am." Uncle Jo wore a clean button-down shirt but refused to take off his trucker hat with Ellie's Diner logo embroidered on it. Since it was brand new from a recent meal there, he insisted it was his best one.

Granny Jo inspected each of us. "It's not often that we have an agent from the International Magic

Patrol come to our house, and I want each of you looking your absolute best."

"Yes, ma'am," I grumbled, suppressing the argument that the agent would come and do his or her business whether we were in good clothes or naked as the day is long.

My father answered the knock on the door and came back to the living room with a scowl. Ebonee followed behind him, wearing a smart pantsuit and tall stilettos.

"Thank you for allowing me to be here for the meeting," she said, regarding each of us. "You all look very fine."

"I called you here as a courtesy to my daughter and out of respect for your position," Dad replied, perching on top of the arm of the couch next to his brother. "Don't think this means I'll be joining your club."

Ebonee raised an eyebrow. "I didn't extend an invitation to you, Buck."

Their banter back and forth gave me the heebie jeebies, and I needed to change the subject fast. "What was the name of the agent?"

"Agent Dryope. Not sure if that's a first name or last," Uncle Jo replied. "All I know is that as soon as we found that IMP marking on the sewing machine, we were obligated to contact their office."

"Does that mean we won't get to sell it for Ms. Robin?" I asked, concerned that the kind woman would get the short end of the stick.

"If the organization doesn't offer reasonable compensation as a finder's fee, then I will take it to the coven to come up with a fair price." Ebonee took out a compact from her purse and reapplied her lipstick.

"That's a kind consideration," Dad remarked, gazing a little too long at her.

I popped up from the chair the moment I heard the second knock. "I'll get it."

A willowy woman with light green hair towered over me. She flashed me a badge. "I'm Agent Dryope of the International Magic Patrol."

Never having met an agent of a large magical organization, I didn't know whether to curtsy, bow, or stare at her.

She cleared her throat. "May I enter?"

"Oh, yes. Please come in." I moved out of her way and marveled at how she almost had to duck to make it through our doorway. "I'm Ruby Mae Jewell, daughter of the person who contacted you."

"I've read a recent report involving you. Seems you were instrumental in taking down a witch who had broken the law and spellbound somebody," she revealed. "That's pretty impressive for someone your age."

When we reached the living room, I looked around at all the people who'd helped me along the way. "I had a lot of help."

"Ruby Mae's an exceptional coven member. I'm Ebonee Johnson, leader of the Crystal Coast Coven." The woman couldn't help but promote herself when she was here to observe.

After introductions to the other members of my family, Dad offered the agent a seat, and she sat down with a lithe grace. "I want to thank you on behalf of IMP for finding Item Number 348K-261 and reporting it. Our agency is prepared to offer you a cash reward for your troubles."

Uncle Jo leaned forward. "It's not so much that we want the money for ourselves, but we'd like to make sure that the lady who thought we were going to sell it for her on consignment gets what it's worth."

"The amount I've been authorized to transfer to you will more than cover a fair price for the object as well as compensate you for your time and effort." Agent Dryope asked for a piece of paper and a pen. She scribbled down some numbers and handed it to my uncle.

He choked on his sip of iced tea when he read the note. "Yeah, that'll more than cover things."

Ebonee shifted in her seat. "I'm glad the agency is willing to treat the local magical community with such respect. But I have to wonder why a large amount of money would be offered for one simple item. What is it about the sewing machine that makes it so valuable?"

For once, I was glad to be the observer and not the instigator when the agent's countenance underneath her leafy-green hair morphed from friendly to shrewd. "Part of the deal would include an agreement that you won't talk about the sewing machine or giving it back to us to anyone after today."

"Sign me up," Uncle Jo exclaimed. "We can finally purchase a new truck to haul things in for that price."

My father placed a hand on his brother's arm. "Nothing good is ever easy. Agent Dryope, before any of us agree to anything, I'd like to echo Ms. Johnson's inquiry. Why all the money? What's the true value of the sewing machine to your agency?"

The green-haired woman leaned back in her chair and crossed her long slender legs. "Fine. But the price of sharing this information is that you will not repeat it."

All of us in the room caved into our curiosity and agreed. The agent crossed her arms as well. "Back in the late sixties, there was a big robbery of IMP holdings when one of our trucks was hijacked. Turns out it was a planned heist involving a couple of rogue agents, so the agency hushed it up to prevent the shame of our failure from being known. Some of the items were recovered, but many of them were sold on the black market and made it out into the mortal world. We've had many teams dispatched to collect and return them back to our vaults."

"I can identify with that," Uncle Jo teased, nudging my father. The joke went over the agent's head.

"From the reports filed with your local wardens, its apparent that the mortal who gained control of the item never realized what she had for her use, and so it went unnoticed for so long." Agent Dryope stood up. "And now I'd like one of you to take me to see it for myself. Before I give you the money, I'd like to verify the item."

Dad glowered at her. "I hope you're not insinuating that you have to make sure we're not fleecing you with a fake."

"I apologize if that's your interpretation of my words," the agent sniffed, failing to truly express an apology.

Uncle Jo stood up. "I've set it up down in our storage barn in preparation for your visit."

"You mean you left it out in the open where anyone could take it?" Agent Dryope scolded.

"We have some pretty decent security," I offered, hoping she'd get a chance to find out for herself just how effective Rex was.

Leaving my father and uncle to take care of the rest, Ebonee prepared to go. "Ruby Mae, I want you to know how pleased I am with all of your work to stop Tara from harming anyone else. I've been informed that Gloria should be released in the next week or so, and that she'll be perfectly clear of any aftereffects of the spellbinding."

A genuine smile spread across my face. "That's good to hear. Thank you for telling me." I escorted her to the door.

She paused before stepping out of the house. "I suppose I've been a little harsher on you than most because of my history with your father." Her braids fell in front of her face as she bent her head. "I guess I would say that being a Jewell isn't a bad thing, and I will no longer imply that." Without looking me in the eyes, she left.

Granny Jo materialized by my side. "Stars in heaven, you better go get a net. Because any moment now, we're gonna see your cousin Deacon flying right past us."

Dad allowed me to give Ms. Robin a good chunk of what we got from the IMP agent. With the official report that Tara had been detained and taken away, the designer embraced her choice to close her shop and finally put together a closeout sale of all of her dresses. She let our close friend group have first choice.

"What do you think?" I asked Dani, holding up a dark green dress in front of my body. "Will this look good on me?"

"I like the dark blue one better," she said, still sorting through the rack to add to her collection.

Crystal called our names and we joined her with Cate on the couch. Azalea and Gloria opened their dressing room curtains at the same time and emerged in gorgeous creations that looked both reminiscent of the stylish past and completely modern.

"I love that yours is the same blush pink," I told the new bride.

Ms. Robin fussed over the fabric. "I had forgotten I had this sweet little number tucked away in the back. And because you lost your other dress, I want you to have this one."

The new bride twisted and turned in the mirror. "I love it. It'll be a perfect dress to wear for our second wedding reception."

Once Roscoe got back from his fishing trip and heard about what happened to Harrison, he wanted to do as much as he could to help them out. In true Roscoe fashion, he provided enough money for them to redo their reception, complete with catered food, cake, and to bring back the band.

Gloria wiped a tear from her eye, happy for her friend. Ms. Robin embraced her by her shoulder. "And if you like what you're wearing, that's yours, too."

We jumped up from the couch with high-pitched squeals and rushed over to gush and rave. I pulled

Ms. Robin off to the side and gave her a long hug. "You didn't have to do that."

She blushed under my attention. "I've got more than enough to last me. I got into the business to make others happy. At least I'm ending things on a good note."

"You definitely are," I agreed, rejoining my friends and accepting a glass of champagne.

After a lot of pain and suffering, we had a lot to celebrate. And because of what we went through, we appreciated moments like this even more.

DEAR READER -

Thanks so much for reading *Rags To Riches,* the second book in the Southern Relics Cozy Mysteries series! If you enjoyed the book (as much as I did writing it), I hope you'll consider leaving a review!

For those who subscribe to my newsletter, you'll get exclusive access to Azalea's and Harrison's Do-Over Reception in the short *You're Invited!*

Preorder Pickup and Pirates and make sure to sign up for my newsletter if you want to hear news and updates!

NEWSLETTER ONLY - If you want to be notified when the next story is released and to get access to exclusive content, sign up for my newsletter! https://www.subscribepage.com/bellafallsrelics

NEWSLETTER & FREE PREQUEL - to gain exclusive access to free shorts and extended stories to my series, go here! https://books.bookfunnel.com/bellasubscriberhextras

Southern Relics Cozy Mysteries

A little sweet
tea and a whole
lot of spells
won't always
put out the fire!

Welcome to Jewell, NC, a small strip of land on the Crystal Coast with no stop signs or traffic lights, but it's got a whole lot of magic. Ruby Mae Jewell helps run the family business of selling antiques and refurbished goods. But with old objects, you never know when one of them possesses more than just dust and cobwebs.

Flea Market Magic

Rags To Witches

Pickup and Pirates

Vintage Vampire (Coming Soon)

Southern Charms
Cozy Mysteries

SOUTHERN CHARMS COZY MYSTERY SERIES

Welcome to Honeysuckle Hollow, the small supernatural Southern town where magic, mystery, and murder make life a real witch for Charli Goodwin. It will take more magic than sweet tea and good food to help her solve murders and save lives.

Suggested reading order:

Chess Pie & Choices: Prequel

Moonshine & Magic: Book 1

Lemonade & Love Potions: A Cozy Short

Fried Chicken & Fangs: Book 2

Sweet Tea & Spells: Book 3

Barbecue & Brooms: Book 4

Collards & Cauldrons: Book 5

Cornbread & Crossroads: Book 6 (Coming Soon)

ACKNOWLEDGMENTS

There are many thanks to be given for this book, but there are some special people I owe this book to.

To all my plot buddies - Melanie Summers, Boyd Craven, Danielle Garrett, Cate Lawley - I would have been in the tall weeds without you lending your ears and your brains to help me crash through the wall.

To the real Crystal, owner of Boro Girl Boutique - Thank you for taking a chance on a local author and featuring my books. I hope you enjoy seeing yourself in my stories!

To my fellow witches from NINC and Salem - You're all amazing, and I'm so happy to fly my broom with you.

And then my family - Without your support, I wouldn't be able to tell the stories that I do.

Last but never least - My Hubs - Your unending support, even when I'm crabby and under a deadline, allows me to soar. Thank you for making sure I eat and drink, and especially for enduring my special brand of crazy.

ABOUT THE AUTHOR

Bella Falls grew up on the magic of sweet tea, barbecue, and hot and humid Southern days. She met her husband at college over an argument of how to properly pronounce the word *pecan* (for the record, it should be *pea-cawn,* and they taste amazing in a pie). Although she's had the privilege of living all over the States and the world, her heart still beats to the rhythm of the cicadas on a hot summer's evening.

Now, she's taken her love of the South and woven it into a world where magic and mystery aren't the only Charms.

bellafallsbooks.com
contact@bellafallsbooks.com

facebook.com/bellafallsbooks
twitter.com/bellafallsbooks
instagram.com/bellafallsbooks
amazon.com/author/bellafalls
bookbub.com/authors/bella-falls

Printed in Great Britain
by Amazon